Also by M. E. Kerr

Dinky Hocker Shoots Smack!
If I Love You, Am I Trapped Forever?
The Son of Someone Famous
Is That You, Miss Blue?

Love
Is a
Missing
Person

An Ursula Nordstrom Book

Harper & Row, Publishers
New York, Evanston, San Francisco, London

Love
Is a
Missing
Person

by M. E. Kerr

The characters and situations in this book are fictional developments and are not meant to portray actual persons.

The lines on page 162 by e.e.cummings are quoted in *The Magic-Maker* by Charles Norman, The Macmillan Company, 1958.

The excerpt from "Healing the Wound" by Heinrich Heine appears in *Heinrich Heine: The Poems* by Louis Untermeyer, copyright, 1937, by Harcourt Brace Jovanovich, Inc.; copyright 1965, by Louis Untermeyer. Reprinted by permission of the publisher.

Library of Congress Catalog Card Number: 75-6299
Trade Standard Book Number: 06-023161-0
Harpercrest Standard Book Number: 06-023162-9
FIRST EDITION

For Evonne Rae
and
Louise Fitzhugh
Missing and Missed

One

It is a Saturday morning and I am writing this at the library.

This is the morning Chicago arrives; no one knows how she'll get here.

It is typical Chicago behavior. My father would charter a plane to bring her here from New York City. He would hire a limousine, a yacht. I think he would even drive her out from the city himself, in all the weekend traffic. But my sister goes out of her way to be independent.

If you have never heard the name Slade, you don't live within thirty miles of Seaville, Long Island, and you've never heard of Continental Office Machines—COM, as they list it on the Big Board.

The first (and last?) boy friend I ever had, two years ago when I was thirteen, once passed a note to me in homeroom. On the outside, for all to see, was my name, written $uzy $lade.

"It's not something to never see me again over," he complained when I caught up with him later at his locker. "I was only teasing."

"It's plenty to never see you again over," I said. "I have

enough of a complex without you rubbing my nose in my grandfather's money!"

"I thought it was your father's," he said.

"My grandfather made it," I said. "My father's just adding to it."

"You should take it in your stride," he said.

"I intend to," I told him, "and I intend to stride right by you from now on."

But I have never been able to take it in my stride. I am not at all like Chicago.

I am not one of your snazzier Slades.

Your snazzier Slades don't even use words like "snazzy" —my mother calls them "tackyisms." I catch words and phrases like other people catch germs, and most of mine originate with Miss Gwendolyn Spring. She is a forty-eight-year-old, self-described nervous wreck, and my favorite friend and ally at the Seaville Free Library.

I am Suzy, the Slade daughter the father chose *not* to take to New York to live with him. My mother actually gave him his choice of girls.

My father's choice was Chicago. Naturally. She was his first-born, his image, his precious. Now, age seventeen, a junior in Abbotsford School, New York City, she is his favorite—blond-haired, blue-eyed, crazy, eccentric, beautiful, beloved.

She's like Daddy, too. She has some showoff in her, as he does. Her nickname resulted from the fact she'd memorized Carl Sandburg's poem about Chicago, one

Christmas when she was just a tyke of five, and done a swaggering rendition of it: "Hog Butcher for the World, Tool Maker, Stacker of Wheat—" et cetera.

She also prizes individuality, as Daddy does. They are a good match.

I, too, have blond hair and blue eyes. I wear glasses for everything. ("Not for your love fantasies, I hope," says Miss Spring when I complain about being a four-eyes. I sneer: "*What* love fantasies!" I have them, though.)

I have the kind of disposition my parents claim their divorce is: an amicable one. I think they're right to make that claim. My mother's never been happier, and Chicago's reports on Daddy's life in New York are always raves. I suppose one reason for that is that they spend all their free time together.

When I see him, he seems the same old daddy, polite and holding back. Around Chicago he's a winker and a feigner of punches to her jaw, as though they are good old buddies with a little secret all their own. They touch a lot and laugh all the time.

When I was younger I used to believe that the little secret was that Daddy made believe she was a boy, because he wanted one so terribly. I was bad at sports; I was an introvert and moper. Chicago could box by the time she was six, and Daddy used to bring her home airplane model kits. They would make them together down in the Tack Room, which is what we Slades call our basement rec room.

According to Miss Spring, my disposition isn't as amicable as it is "as yet unformed," and "amicable divorces are always easier when there's a lot of money."

I used to play down the money thing as much as I could, when I first became a volunteer at the library. I also told Miss Spring what I considered to be the truth: "My life isn't that much easier than anyone else's."

"How would you know what anyone else's is like?" she answered. "You live in a cocoon, Mama-doodle!" She looked up at me with those wild eyes almost blurred out of existence behind whirls of glass like the bottoms of Coke bottles. Owl Eyes, some call her. She has frizzy yellow hair and stands a little over five foot three, and though almost all the librarians are into slacks at least a few days a week, Miss Spring's costumes here never vary. She wears a skirt and sweater and saddle shoes and white socks. She always smells of Tweed perfume, and sometimes under her sweaters she wears these round white collars, biblike affairs with no sleeves, called "dickeys," popular, my mother told me, "back in World War II when Gwendolyn Spring was *not* popular."

I'd ask, "Why wasn't she popular?"

"She wasn't with the *girls*, anyway," my mother'd say, and I wouldn't pursue the subject. Do you understand? I wouldn't let her get the knife in again for another twist.

Question, apropos of nothing in particular to do with this subject, or Chicago: Why is my mother, who is still

4

beautiful, who married well, who divorced well, who smiles around all day complimenting the maids and the cook and the gardener on how well they're taking care of her—WHY is she determined to slander poor Gwendolyn Spring (who hasn't had a fourth of her luck in life) smack in the middle of a description about "dickeys"?

Anyway, back to Miss Spring's description of my life, inside a cocoon.

"I'm not that sheltered!" I argued back.

"Oh, honey," a new voice chimed in, "you don't know nothin' out there on Ocean Road. Out there on Ocean Road you in Dream City!"

That was Nan Richmond putting in her two cents, slipping into the black vernacular she gets into whenever we're all clowning around at the library. She gets into it when she's mad, too.

Nan is a chocolate-colored black, age sixteen, a junior at school. She lives in Inscape, a part of Seaville near the bay, where the artists' settlement is on one side, and the black settlement is on the other.

Nan is a page at the library, the first black page Seaville ever hired.

The day before she arrived, Mrs. Timberlake, head librarian, took me aside and in her best and most professional library whisper, said to me, "The colored like to be called black, dear, so try not to slip. We want her to feel right at home. . . . I don't know what was so bad about the word Negro."

I said, "I go to school with blacks, Mrs. Timberlake. Don't worry about it."

"Then you must help me to understand her," said Mrs. Timberlake.

"There's nothing special to understand," I said a little resentfully. "I'm not exactly going to school with cannibals or any other exotic species."

"*Dear,*" she said, "we are taking on a black for the precise reason that we feel one will be a most worthwhile addition to our staff. . . . All I meant about your going to school with blacks is that Seaville High is almost 30 per cent black now. The same thing that happened in Oceanside could happen here."

All the adults worry that we'll turn into Oceanside. Its high school is 80 per cent black.

Nan says that's what we get for hauling all her ancestors up from down South for cheap labor generations ago. We should have left well enough alone, Nan says, and if we had wanted to keep our future schools lily-white, then our great-great-grandparents should have hired some white hands to scrub down the floors and haul trash, and cook and clean and break their backs pulling potatoes out of the ground.

Nan's got a mouth on her and she uses it often.

I was complaining once about having to work in the library for nothing, so I could get my allowance (a rule of my mother's, so I'll be out of her way afternoons).

"Oh, honey, honey, honey," Nan piped up, "I'd like to die imagining you without your allowance, child. No more tape decks, huh? No more of those funsy, second-hand World War II clothes from Outlet, hmmm? No more two-dollar hot fudge sundaes from Sweet Mouth, ah? Lord take pity on you, without your 'lowance, you gonna be reduced to poverty level."

My answer to her was to go light up one of her cigarettes back in the staff room, show the world how bright she is, sucking on poison every half hour. I told her she spent her money so much more wisely than I did, buying cancer for herself in little cellophane packages!

Mrs. Timberlake once said, "I can always tell when you and Nan aren't working, because Nan starts that Negro-style talk."

"Black-style," I said. "Remember?"

"I do admire Nan, though," Mrs. Timberlake always added, fearful she would be accused of a racial slur if she suggested Nan was goofing off. "She gives her all to us."

The fact is neither Nan nor I really give our all. Nan wants to be a songwriter, that's *her* impossible dream, and mine is to be a newspaper reporter who interviews all sorts of people. Nan works on her lyrics, and I read profiles and biographies, practice my writing, and add words to my vocabulary.

Right this minute as I look up from my journal, I am watching Nan, and listening to her talking with her boy friend.

His name is Roger Coe III. He's a black-black, not chocolate-colored like Nan, and he's got blue eyes, which is not too common. He's six foot, weighs 180 pounds, according to the football program, and he's a halfback, captain of the Seaville High Salts, who were last year undefeated.

Roger is also a track, baseball, and tennis star, and a pole-vaulter.

He is also a straight-A student.

Roger is another one who, if you haven't heard of him, you don't live within thirty miles of Seaville, Long Island, New York.

I think he could be a movie star.

Sample of their conversation, practically word for word:

NAN: So I'll see you tonight?

ROGER: Look deep at me, not away.

(This embarrasses Nan. She shakes her head and looks toward the ceiling. Roger doesn't smile or anything, just stares at her hard.)

NAN: Don't fool around Roger. You're not even supposed to be in this place this hour of day.

ROGER: This is a public place. Look deep, honey. See what you find in my eyes.

NAN: Oh, man. Oh, crazy, man. (She's more embarrassed.)

ROGER: Here now, see you smile.

Now he reaches to touch her face and she pushes his hand away and he puts it back. She pushes it away again and gives him a small shove. They keep this up, starting to laugh, acting crazy.

Miss Spring says sometimes being in love is a form of

craziness. She says sometimes being in love elevates you to the realms of insanity.

I asked her once if she meant the kind of love Nan and Roger have.

"No," she said, "their love is sweet. It's tender. It's someday-we'll-probably-get-married love, and it's fun to watch. . . . But it's not exalting to watch."

"It's not what?" I said.

"It's not exalting to watch," she said.

That's what I thought she said, but I didn't know exactly what she meant.

I asked my mother and my mother said women like Gwendolyn Spring, who had to go around watching other people in love, would never know the meaning of the word exalting.

"When do you feel exalted?" I said.

"Sunday mornings when I sing in the choir," she answered. "That's one time. There are other times. They're personal."

"At least Gwendolyn Spring tells me things," I said.

"Who else has she got to talk to?" my mother said.

We don't enjoy the closest mother/daughter relationship in the world.

I was just interrupted.

"Mama-doodle," Miss Spring said, "your sister's outside waiting to talk to you. I'll take over the desk while you're gone."

"My sister's *here*?"

"On a motorcycle, Mama-doodle."

"Chicago doesn't own a motorcycle," I said.

"Quit stalling, quit writing in that notebook, quit acting like a zombie, and get out there," said Miss Spring. "She's your own sister."

Now that I know how she got here, I wonder why she came.

Two

"Where did you get that thing?" I said, without saying Hello, Chicago, or How are you, Chicago? I folded my arms across my chest and stood there in front of the library, looking down at the ground and up at my sister out of the corner of my eye.

Chicago was sitting on the motorcycle, most of her face covered by goggles that were attached to a white crash helmet with C. Slade written across it in red ink.

"I just got in a few minutes ago," she said.

"Where did you get that?" I said.

"Dad bought it for me. It's a Harley 145."

She smiled at me and I looked away, embarrassed.

"Get on the back," she said.

"You crazy, Chicago?"

"I already asked Miss Saddle Shoes if you could take a coffee break."

"I don't drink coffee," I said, "and she doesn't have any authority over me."

"She said you could. I bet nothing ever happens Saturdays in there, anyway."

"Chicago," I said, wishing we weren't right there in full view on Main Street with her decked out like some guy from a motorcycle gang, "I'm afraid of motorcycles."

"You're afraid of too many things, Suzy. At least clear up your fear of motorcycles, and then you can begin to attack the rest."

"*What?*" I said. "I don't have any obsessive fear of motorcycles that's preventing me from having a normal life or anything like that. I don't want to get on the back of that thing."

She said, "You're absolutely right."

I said with astonishment, "I am?"

She unstrapped her crash helmet and pulled it off her head, along with the goggles.

She was still wearing her hair in almost a Marine boot's cut, and getting away with it, as some exotic *Vogue* model might. Chicago has a fantastic face. She has deep-blue eyes and a great wide white smile, and soft skin usually tanned from the sun, in any season.

"Here." She held out the helmet.

"I don't want it. Why?"

"Because you're going for a ride with me, somewhere for just a few minutes where we have total privacy."

I looked closely at her. She wasn't wearing one of her

con-artist smiles or giving me the business in any way whatsoever. Chicago was serious. I can't remember ever having seen such a solemn expression on her face.

It frightened me somewhat.

I said, "If anyone died, I don't want to be told about it at the end of a motorcycle ride."

"No one died," she said, "but something *is* dead."

"Something that was alive once?"

"Very much alive," said Chicago. "A way of life."

"Has Daddy lost his money or something?"

"Suzy," Chicago said, "you're like some little kid who's afraid to step out of the house until she knows exactly what's going on, and if she'll be absolutely safe. My advice is to get your ass out the door and take your chances like everyone else. You're not five years old anymore!"

"Okay," I agreed, reaching out to take the helmet from her hand, "but why does it involve getting on the back of some machine that could slam into a truck?"

"I'll be the one to get killed or suffer the brain concussion," she said. "I'm letting you wear the helmet."

"You were always all heart, Chicago."

"I wouldn't suggest this if it wasn't absolutely necessary, Suzy."

"You'd suggest it if it wasn't absolutely necessary," I said. "You've always been dramatic."

"*Was*," said Chicago. "Past tense. Former life."

I fixed the helmet on my head and pulled down the goggles. Then I slung my leg over the back of the bike and mounted the rear seat. I just hoped Miss Spring was looking out the window, beginning to regret ever telling my sister I was free for a break. I half-hoped she'd see the imminent disaster and come running out, screaming that I couldn't leave the library grounds . . . whether or not she had any authority over me.

The other half of me was really curious about what Chicago had on her mind.

I decided if Daddy had lost all his money, I'd get a summer job waitressing out at Tout Va Bien. I'd lie about my age. By fall I'd be sixteen, old enough to drop out of school and get a full-time job.

Chicago began to hit the starter pedal with her foot, trying to get the engine to kick over.

"What am I going to hang on to?" I shouted at her.

"Me," she answered.

I felt as doomed as someone with ESP New York-bound on the *Titanic*. Who in her right mind would hang on to Chicago for support?

The Hadefield Club is right on the ocean, about two miles down the road from our house. You can park next to it, in this public area reserved for village residents who pay twelve dollars for a blue sticker. Off season very few people go there, though there are always a certain amount curious to see the Hadefield in any season. They just go there and stare at it, like tourists in Hollywood who ride around following a map of stars' homes, never seeing more than gates and shrubbery and trees and lawns.

At the Hadefield you can see the extensive golf course and tennis courts and the clubhouse and the rows of cabanas.

A long time ago my family was invited to join, which is viewed by many in Seaville as some sort of privilege. My father always left things like memberships up to my mother, and my mother said she would rather join the W.C.T.U. than the Hadefield. Quite a statement for a woman who likes her bourbon as well as I like my Häagen-Dazs ice cream.

My mother calls the Hadefield the Hatefilled. The reason the Slades never joined is because up until five years ago the Hatefilled would not allow Jews, and my mother would not belong to a club so bigoted. When Jews were finally admitted, it was arranged by a quota system which permitted only a few, all carefully screened and hand-picked by the board of directors. My mother says it's just tokenism, that it's the same old Hatefilled.

Chicago stopped right in front of the Hadefield, and shut off the motor.

"I wish it was in season," she said, "so I could shake up those stupid jackasses in that place with a little noise and dust."

"People aren't going to like you driving this thing around Seaville," I said, wondering if I could still walk after that terror ride down Fouracre Path. I could. I

14

walked up to the dunes while Chicago put the bike up on its stand.

I heard Chicago yell something like, "Seaville's going to have to get used to me," but I wasn't sure that was it, exactly. There was a strong wind and the ocean had a wild look with great crashing waves and plenty of whitecaps.

"Let's walk along the ocean," said Chicago as she came up behind me.

I jumped. Chicago always walks like an Indian; you never hear her coming. She walks in secret, the way she thinks and plans and dreams.

I said, "Let's just sit down here on the dune." I got a funny image of Chicago tossing me in, trying to drown me—I don't know—not a serious feeling she would, but around Chicago I always felt threatened by something.

I told my mother this and she said, "Well, I don't want to sound like that shrink I paid an average man's life's earnings to, but maybe what really bothers you is how *you* feel about Chicago."

I didn't like it when anyone reminded me how I felt about my sister. I didn't like not liking Chicago. I said, "That doesn't make any sense." Even though it did. I sensed that it did.

Mother said, "It's not unusual for people to reverse feelings they're not comfortable with. For example: Maybe I think I was unfair to your dad about something. So what I do with it is say that he's accusing me of being unfair . . . *or* accuse him of being unfair. See, Suzy?"

I saw, but I preferred not to face it. I couldn't face deep subjects with my mother. Our own relationship was too shallow.

I said, "Oh, psychology makes an orchid farm out of a simple little dandelion patch."

"Quite a compliment to psychology."

"And it also makes a vast mathematical problem out of two and two."

"What's your idea of two and two?" said my mother.

"What do you mean, what's my idea of two and two?"

"What is your idea of two and two?"

"Four," I said. "What's yours?"

"Four," she said. "Sometimes. . . . And sometimes it's twenty-two."

That's Evelyn Slade for you. Nothing is ever simple, including simple arithmetic. Maybe that's why we don't get along famously. I like simple explanations and simple reactions and simple pleasures.

Back to Chicago and me, still standing on the dunes.

"Okay," she said sitting down, "have it your way. We'll sit."

"I haven't got all day, either," I said. I wasn't used to intimacy with Chicago. I had the feeling she was going to say something too personal for her to tell me. I was thinking that Chicago should be the last person in the family to break any important news to me.

"Then I'll get right to the point, Suzy. I'm asking a favor of you."

"Are you in trouble?"

"It's the most important favor I'll ever ask you."

"You're not pregnant?"

"Suzy, I want to change places. I want to live with Mom from now on, and you live with Dad."

"Me move to New York?"

"You've always preferred Dad, anyway."

"But Daddy prefers you."

"Dad agrees to this, Suzy. We've talked about it."

"I don't know anyone in New York, Chicago!"

"I don't really know anyone here, either."

"Daddy prefers you."

"Dad loves us both, Suzy."

"I don't want to live with him just because you decided it. He didn't decide it."

"He's delighted."

"*Delighted!*" I said sarcastically. "That's Mom's word for something really phony."

"I'm going to start school here in Seaville on Monday. Dad arranged it."

"This late in the year? You must be really determined!"

"Don't worry, Suzy, we're not steamrolling you into anything. You finish ninth grade, and then, if you want to, you start tenth in New York at Abbotsford . . . or anywhere you want to go."

"What does Mother say?"

"She'll agree," Chicago said. "Don't you know by now that Mother would agree to anything Dad says?"

I couldn't think of anything to say to that.

"I've got to get out from under Dad's thumb, Suzy. He's smothering me."

For some reason, that confession embarrassed me. I guess because I could imagine the truth behind it. I'd seen Daddy with Chicago sometimes when you'd think they were lovers instead of father and daughter. I don't mean anything bad by that, but sometimes Daddy just laughs too hard at something Chicago says that's not funny. Sometimes he watches her as though she's some sort of marvel he can't believe is real. Sometimes he tells things she's done that aren't unusual, except he makes it sound phenomenal. Chicago is enough of an individual without all the fanfare from Daddy, but Daddy can't seem to stop.

I told Chicago, "I like living in a small town."

"You don't get along that well with Mother, do you?"

"We manage."

"Suzy, I'm about to crack up if I don't get away from Dad. He's trying to run my life. He clocks me in and out. He criticizes my friends. Now that I'm almost legally an adult, it's worse than ever. I think he's jealous of my friends, and of any life I have that he's not included in."

"*Daddy?*" I said with some surprise, because it sounded pretty heavy even for him. "How come he's willing to let you live here then?"

Chicago heaved a sigh. "Suzy, it's very complicated. I just hope you'll back me up when I tell Mom."

"Don't *I* have any time to think about it?"

"You've got until fall before you have to make the move."

"Chicago," I said, "I don't *have* to do anything."

I wasn't sure of that, but I decided to use a forceful tack. Around Chicago it's important not to lose any ground.

Three

Sometimes Roger Coe III likes to get off these smart remarks in rhyme. Nan says it's not original with Roger, it's a thing some blacks like to do to jive you, or because they think it's cool.

I'm glad Roger deigns to notice me at all, even though I know it's because I'm Nan's friend from the library. The ninth grade is nowhere enough, and in Seaville it's worse because it's your first year at Seaville Senior High. S.S.H. doesn't have out any welcome mat for freshmen.

We are the lowest of the low, too young to drive or drink, and in some places in the town of Seaville they won't even sell cigarettes to anyone under eighteen. I don't care about cigarettes, but I wish ninth graders were noticed more by someone besides other ninth graders.

Roger Coe III never looks away when he sees me coming, and he never looks right through me like some seniors. He's always got a smile and something to say, and if it's been a rotten day up until then, it's less rotten. Roger's Someone at S.S.H., and that helps, too. If you feel as crummy as I do 60 per cent of the time, it gives you a lift to have a celebrity notice you. Particularly on a Monday, in the morning.

I was on my way from third period, which is Social Studies. The kids call it "a map and a movie a day." We'd just seen the last of the Dr. Ethel J. Apenfels slides, an in-depth study of Japan. I was moping along the hall with Martha Crammer, when Roger came around the corner and stopped in his tracks, as though he was seeing a ghost. He's a clown, Roger is, and he'll go into a whole act for an audience of two.

"Well, hi there, Suzy Q. How you?"

"Hi, Roger."

"A girl with the name of a city, looks like a boy—what a pity."

At first I didn't think I'd heard him right, but I saw Martha hunch over and catch her mouth with her palm, keeping herself from laughing. Martha said, "Chicago," and Roger said, "is in Illinois," and the two of them laughed, bent double.

"Do you both have perfect relatives?" I managed to say.

Roger said, "I got an aunt who wears drag and shaves her face. Her name's Leonard."

Martha doubled up with laughter a second time, as Roger gave a two-fingered salute and sauntered away.

Finally Martha said, "Your sister's not anything like you, Suzy."

"My sister's almost beautiful," I said.

"She's a little tough, isn't she?"

"She's original."

"Oh, is that the word for it?"

"You wouldn't know someone who was original if you fell over her," I said.

"Lena Klein's original."

"She's creative," I said, "but not really original."

Martha said, "What's the difference?"

I gave a long exasperated sigh to stall for thinking time, and then I said, "You really don't know the difference between creative and original?" I was hoping hard that I could come up with something.

Martha shook her head.

"Creative has to create," I said. "Original doesn't have to do anything. It's enough to be!"

Martha looked impressed.

It wasn't a bad answer, particularly when it comes to Chicago.

I'm writing this in homeroom, and if I have enough time, I'll give you an illustration of why that definition suits my sister, as well as a small glimpse of our weekend.

It started in a lot of ways: with this big embrace between my mother and Chicago, as though they both really meant it, which surprised me and hurt me, too. My mother and I barely graze cheeks when we are in some situation which requires us to show physical affection. I've always told myself that she has trouble being demonstrative. But there they were, like two old college roomies, hugging hard, with actual tears in my mother's eyes.

It also started with a phone call from my father, asking to speak with Chicago first, to which Chicago responded with a flat "No!" She didn't speak to him at all. Mother babbled away for a while and I got trapped into a promise that I'd go into New York City for a weekend in two weeks.

It got started with Chicago asking if we'd share my room, or if she was being banished to her old room—now another guest room in the back of the house, minus an ocean view. What could I say? I had to clear out my library, which is what I called the other twin bed in my room. I piled all my books there, and it was my desk as well.

But the weekend really started after dinner. My mother made herself a bourbon and told us to come out to the solarium and watch the moon come up. She pushed the windows open so we could hear the ocean and smell the salt air, and she stuck a cassette in the tape recorder. For no good reason that I could figure out, it was one of those selected subject tapes. The subject was joy. It began with a rousing chorus from Beethoven's Ninth.

Mother sat in the white wicker chair with the yellow cushions, looking very Better-Homes-and-Gardensy since she was wearing a long yellow dress made of some flimsy

22

material, and yellow sandals. Mother has yellow hair, more or less. It's streaked by a beauty parlor in Oceanside.

The ghost of Mother is leaning over my shoulder making corrections. (Can a live person have a ghost?) She is telling me that a beauty parlor does not do someone's hair, a person does. She is telling me that the phrase "beauty parlor" is a vulgarism, that I should simply refer to the hairdresser, say that she visits the hairdresser in Oceanside.

Mother is a good-looking woman, the sort who's always tanned in March and volunteering all over the place in the spring, to make up for the fact she wintered in Acapulco. She's the type who uses the word "community responsibility" habitually, and who once every other week rolls bandages or licks envelopes for the Red Cross, while Macaulay waits outside for her in the Lincoln limousine.

She's the type men turn around to look at, and she's always pretending I imagine it. Or she says something really humiliating to me like, "He was probably turning around to look at you. You're growing up, you know." Remarks like that make me want to barf. I'll know when some grown man's head is swiveling around to catch another glimpse of me ... and I hope by then I'll have outgrown my 32-A Maidenform.

Mother was in the white wicker chair, studying the light against the glass of ice cubes with the I.W. Harper poured over them, as though she was admiring some subtle and prized mosaic.

23

I was wearing a caftan and espadrilles, thumbing through the new Hammacher Schlemmer catalogue. I stopped at an item called a Surf and Rain Sleep Sound, a machine which promised to reproduce the sound of ocean wave patterns, and sold for seventy-five dollars.

Chicago was in a pair of men's khaki pants, a white shirt rolled up at the sleeves, and on her feet, a pair of old high top black-and-white sneakers. She was sitting on the windowsill looking out at the view.

"First of all," my mother began, and I knew there was going to be a lecture. "First of all," she repeated, because Chicago was still looking at the view and not my mother, "I think we ought to come to an agreement. Is that something you go along with, Chicago?"

"Sure." Chicago looked at her long enough to smile, and then looked back to the ocean.

"Even Jackson Pollack proved that he could draw and paint in recognizable fashion before he took up a career of throwing paint at a canvas."

I tore my eyes from the catalogue copy of the Surf and Rain Sleep Sound to try to fathom from a glance at my mother's face what direction she was traveling in.

Chicago was giving my mother her full attention now, too.

Chicago said, "Meaning what?"

"Meaning that I would like you to appear occasionally in public in feminine apparel, merely to prove that you are familiar with both ways of dressing, but have *chosen* one direction more than the other."

"I don't own a dress," Chicago said.

"Well, you will very soon," said my mother.

"Owning something isn't wearing something," said Chicago.

"Living here isn't living freely," my mother said.

Chicago looked surprised. "Isn't it?"

"No. Living here is living with people and respecting their opinions and feelings."

"Why don't you let your hair grow, too?" I said.

My mother said, "Suzy, tais-toi!" That's what the French say instead of "Ferme la bouche," when they want to say "shut up!" politely.

Chicago said, "If I *appear* in these clothes, I have obviously *chosen* these clothes, n'est-ce pas?"

"I want people in Seaville to know you know the difference."

That argument lasted for the length of time it took the moon to rise, and we were sitting in the dark when my mother began to cry.

"All *right*!" Chicago said. The joy tape was playing Bach's "Jesu, Joy of Man's Desiring."

My mother recovered immediately and issued another directive. "Suzy is never to ride on your motorcycle again."

"All right," Chicago mumbled.

"You are not to ride your motorcycle to school."

There were a lot of rules, one after the other once Chicago had given in to my mother on the first condition, and that was Chicago's mistake, I figured.

Mother had more bourbon, and seemed to delight in

25

making up still more rules. Be in by ten week nights. Announce your destination. Introduce the friends you make. Blah blah blah blah blah et cetera. Mother was getting drunk with power on I.W. Harper.

It was a dumb Saturday night, sitting in the dark in the solarium while Mother got a little thick-tongued and awfully bossy.

When Chicago and I were undressing for bed, I said, "You were really good-natured about Mother's laws."

"I wasn't good-natured," she said. "I'm just not involved with them."

"How do you figure?"

"Most of them are about going places and doing things. I'm not interested in any of that."

"What are you interested in, Chicago?"

"In leveling," she said.

"You mean being honest, saying what's on your mind?"

"That, too. But I mean literally leveling: getting things level.... Do you ever wonder why we have it so good and some families can't even afford to eat meat?"

"Sure, I've thought of it."

"I have too, a lot," said Chicago. "I almost became a revolutionary because of a boy named Scott McKay, but his family sent him off to military school. Boy, did Dad hate him."

"Why?"

"He was an anarchist."

"That's why Daddy hated him?"

"That's part of why," she said.

"What's the other part?"

"Does it matter?" Her voice had actually cracked and there were what almost looked like tears in her eyes. She turned her face away from me.

"Don't you want to talk about it?" I said.

"I'm tired of talking about, thinking about, having my whole world revolve about Dad."

"Okay," I said. "Forget it."

"Everyone around here is too fat!" Chicago snapped.

"Fat?" I weighed 105 pounds.

"Too selfish and too spoiled!" Chicago said. "No one feels very deeply."

I shut my eyes after I stretched out on my bed. I felt slightly put down by Chicago.

Eventually I said, "Sometimes late at night if I'm not in bed, it just means I'm walking down by the ocean. I do a lot of thinking that way."

She didn't answer me. She didn't even hear me, and I'd said it just to impress her. I thought she'd think it was deep.

She was almost talking to herself. "People only want to see their own version of you, not the real you. Parents never want to see the real you."

I put out the light.

I said, "Chicago? Did you love Scott McKay?"

"That's a revolting thought. He only came up to my chin, and any strong wind could have blown him away."

"I was just trying to figure out the other part of why Daddy hated him," I said.

"Because he was wise to Dad. He was the first one to clue me in on Dad."

"Clue you in how?"

"Clue me in that Dad didn't love me. He just loved possessing me. I was just another possession."

"Then why didn't he love possessing me?"

"Oh, shut up, Suzy, I don't want to talk about him. I *don't*!"

"Well, don't get angry," I said. "But it's a fact he chose you and he didn't choose me, and we're both his possessions."

"I am *not* Dad's possession!" she said adamantly. "Good night!"

The next morning I walked home from church with my mother.

"Did you feel exalted when you sang this morning?" I asked.

"Lay off, Suzy. You know I have a hangover."

"Isn't Chicago going to join us Sunday mornings?"

"I want to think about it for a while," my mother said. "Suzy, did she tell you anything about her reason for moving out here?"

"No," I said. I wasn't going to give away Chicago's confidences.

"All this business about Daddy smothering her. I don't

believe that," said my mother, who apparently was in on the same confidence I was in on. "It isn't your father's style at all, to smother anyone. He *is* a loving man, a very loving man . . . but he wouldn't smother anyone."

I felt as though something was stuck in my throat. It was probably the idea of my father as a loving man. I preferred to think he was a cold fish, except when it came to Chicago.

I said to Mother, "You're glad she's here, aren't you?" If she answered yes, I knew it meant she was glad I was going to live with Daddy. I held my breath.

My mother shook her head. "It isn't that easy."

At least my mother is consistent. Was anything ever easy for her?

Homeroom is almost over. Word is spreading that Kelly Plante is outside with her baby. She's Kelly Plante Dix now. She married a black named Lionel Dix and they both dropped out of school last year. Everyone's asking what color the baby is, but nobody's seen her yet.

Martha Crammer's mother said Kelly Plante ruined her life, and there'll be more like her because Seaville High's going the way of Oceanside.

Nan Richmond said the next time a Kelly Plante goes after a black guy, a whole gang of females from Inscape are going to beat in her little white head.

The bell.

Four

The library pages and junior volunteers are not supposed to go near the Phineas Ulin Collection. It's kept in the attic of the Seaville Free Library, where Gwendolyn Spring's office is.

Very few Seavillers have easy access to the collection. No one under eighteen does.

Phineas Ulin collected thousands of books, most extremely rare and all valuable. The subject matter of these books is officially catalogued as "erotica." My mother would describe it as pornography. Mrs. Timberlake calls it "filth." I guess a lot of people in Seaville agree with Mrs. Timberlake, since it's most often called the P-*U* Collection.

In his will, Phineas Ulin also bequeathed a yearly stipend to be paid to the librarian in charge of his collection. The board of directors probably would have found a man to do the job, except that Phineas Ulin made it very clear that it was to be a "broad-minded, sensitive female not over forty years of age when she undertakes the assignment."

The only woman in Seaville who applied for the job was Miss Spring, although librarians from all over sent in applications. Miss Spring has been in charge of the P-*U* collection for some twenty-six years now.

People have been known to travel from abroad to see certain pieces in the collection, and Miss Spring's correspondence concerning it is the most mail the library gets.

I'll get back to the P-U collection in a minute.

Chicago's been with us now for nearly ten days, and I've been late getting to the library afternoons. She always waits for me after the last bell, and then wants to have a conversation with me about classes and the kids and the teachers. She's got me feeling sorry for her because she's such a loner.

By the time I straggle into the library, every cart in the place is jammed with books to be put back on the shelves.

Today when I arrived here, late again, I could see Nan at the desk, her mouth twitching slightly as it does when she's trying not to burst out laughing. I thought she was being mean, because Mrs. Timberlake was furious with me. Mrs. Timberlake was sitting at her desk with her glasses down on the tip of her nose, watching me above the panes. She didn't take her eyes off me until I got four carts unloaded.

When she finally went back to the staff room, I walked up to the desk where Nan was working at Check Out.

"Can they fire a volunteer?" I said.

"Suzy," she skipped past my question, "we happen to be faced with a golden opportunity. The big G.O., Suzy."

"Is that what you've been smiling at since I've come in?"

"Miss Spring is sick, Suzy, and she left at noon. Old Owl Eyes forgot to lock the gate." Nan gave a hoot and clapped her hand across her mouth. "Pulled it, but did not lock it.

Latched it, but did not lock it. Left, but did not lock it."
She gave me a big wink and a little goose which made me
jump.

A few times when I'd been up talking with Miss Spring
I'd seen glimpses of the collection. I saw some old engravings she was patching; they were a grouping titled something like "The Sultan and His Five Hundred Wives." I'd
also seen bits of poetry copied across drawing paper with
water-color illustrations. Phineas Ulin often hired an artist
named Fabrizio to illustrate certain poetry he liked. The
Fabrizios were the most valuable pieces in the collection.
Fabrizio had become a famous painter and then put a bul-
let through his brain at the peak of his success.

Miss Spring said Fabrizio had tasted the greatest of life's
adventures—the fulfillment of his reason for living—and
he had gone on to the next life, and the adventures there.

My mother said Fabrizio was an Inscape gin drinker,
and all gin-drinking artists are melancholics. My mother
said if there hadn't been a loaded gun in the house, he
would probably be around today, complaining that he
didn't have enough recognition.

(The loaded gun was because Fabrizio was always trying to scare away the squirrels and raccoons from his corn
garden.)

Nan said she was going to get a ten-minute break in
about two minutes, and we could sneak up to the attic together.

I figured what if I did get caught, get fired, have my allowance taken away. If I was going to New York City to live, none of it would matter anyway.

"We're going to see all those dirty things, Suzy." Nan put her arms around herself and gave herself a little hug.

"Sexy things," I corrected her.

"Oh, honey, what's the difference between the two!" she laughed. "Don't be so busy trying to clean up sex or you're going to spoil it." She gave another laugh. Anything to do with the subject of sex always got Nan acting about four years younger than she was.

I said, "What I know about the subject you could pour down an ant's throat, and have room left for how much I adore my sister."

"I'll meet you up there—you go ahead," Nan said. Then she added, "Yeah, you got a lunatic there for kin. Loony tunes."

I walked down through the stacks wondering why I always had to do that lately: make sure I got in at least a dig a day about my sister. I didn't even wait for the subject of my sister to come up, lately. I just went right at her, with a typical little remark like I'd made to Nan.

I wondered if I was becoming like my mother that way. Once when my father was really angry with her, he said she was one of the most "gratuitously mean" women he had ever known. I never forgot that phrase, and often when my mother went out of her way to make some snide remark about someone, I thought of it.

The staircase leading up to Miss Spring's office was a

narrow, winding one. The office was in a cramped corner by a window which looked out on the gardens of the Crammer estate. Martha Crammer's home was never called a home or a house or an address or even the Crammer place. It was always the Crammer estate. Her grandfather had invented something to do with airplane machinery, and their estate went from the library all the way down Main Street to Patchin Place. That's a lot of acres.

On Miss Spring's desk there was a photograph of Lester Quinn, Miss Spring's old beau, in his World War II uniform, when he flew a B-29. He was smiling, too baby-faced to be dropping bombs on people, I always thought when I saw him. He'd written across the bottom, "For Gwen, my love, all ways, always." That made Nan giggle whenever she saw it. I'd say, "Why?"

"It's the double meaning. The big D.M., Suzy!"

"But so what?"

"You are such a child you belong in the Children's Room hearing the mouse stories and the elephant tales."

"You're the child. Sex is a perfectly natural thing." I'd rather die than admit I didn't have the slightest idea whether or not what I was saying was true. Somehow I doubted it very much.

But we'd tease each other, and never really agree on the subject of sex, love, and marriage. Nan said I was a dreamer like Miss G. Spring and then she'd hoot at the idea that G. Spring sounded like G. String, and she'd slip

34

into some stripper routine, snapping her fingers and saying, "Oh, take it off, Gwendolyn."

In most ways, Nan was more together than all of the kids I went to school with. She had solid plans. Because Roger would graduate a year ahead of her, he'd go on to engineering school while she was doing her senior year. Then they'd get married, and Nan would go back to college with him. She'd work and help him through, though Roger was bound to get some kind of scholarship.

Nan was mostly serious; it was just that real personal things made her silly.

I wasn't surprised when I suddenly heard this muffled giggling as I felt her looking over my shoulder, at a Fabrizio I'd found on Miss Spring's desk.

I'm not going to describe what Fabrizio had painted, except to say it was a man and a woman, and they were making love. The interesting thing was that it was an illustration of a poem by Emily Dickinson, called "Wild Nights." Funny, because I always thought of her as just this proper New England lady who'd never married.

This is the poem:

> Wild nights! Wild nights!
> Were I with thee,
> Wild nights should be
> Our luxury!
>
> Futile the winds
> To a heart in port—

Done with the compass
Done with the chart.

Rowing in Eden.
Ah! the sea!
Might I but moor
Tonight in thee!

"Come on!" Nan said. "Let's look at some of the other
stuff."

"Okay," I said. But I didn't move. I put the Fabrizio on
Miss Spring's desk, where I'd found it. Then I stood there
a moment and reread the poem. Sometimes I have to read
a poem a few times to understand it. Sometimes when I
finally did understand a poem, I really ached because I
would never be able to think up anything as lovely as a line
like "Futile the winds to a heart in port."

" 'Seventeenth-Century Brothels!' " I heard Nan exclaim
behind me.

She brought a large book of engravings across to me
and said, "Look! Two women together!"

"Haven't you heard of that?"

"Heard it but not seen it," she said.

"The important things are supposed to be back in the big
green file," I said. "It's Oriental stuff."

I'd heard Miss Spring say to visitors that the Eastern part
of the collection was the most "original." I was positive
that I knew what she meant by the word "original" in ref-
erence to the P-_U_ collection.

Nan was starting back toward the file when I heard Mrs. Timberlake's voice call out, "Who is up there?"

She was making her way up the winding stairs.

Nan ducked behind the green file.

Suddenly, Mrs. Timberlake and I were face to face. "What are you doing up here, Suzy?"

"I came up to get something for Miss Spring."

"What?"

"What?"

"What were you getting for Miss Spring?"

I reached across and picked up the photograph of Lieutenant Lester Quinn.

"This, ma'am," I said. "She feels better if she has it, particularly when she's home ill."

Mrs. Timberlake shook her head and made a clucking sound. "When is that woman going to perceive the fact Lester Quinn has been someone else's husband for twenty-five years now!"

"I don't know," I said. I was sure my heart was beating hard enough for Mrs. Timberlake to see it pushing through my sweater.

"Bring it along, then, and we'll lock up. She forgot to lock up. I'll go up front and get my keys."

I followed her down the stairs. I could hear Nan coming along not far behind me, but not near enough for Mrs. Timberlake to see.

"Oh, by the way," Mrs. Timberlake said over her shoulder. "Your father called and left a number for you to call.

He's staying at Seaville Manor. Doesn't he stay with your mother when he comes out?"

He always did, but I wasn't about to show my surprise to Mrs. Timberlake.

I tried to sound totally nonchalant. "My mother's taken up with our chauffeur," I said.

"Suzy!"

Then she got even with me for shocking her. Mrs. Timberlake can always go you one better. She said, "I think I'd better give Miss Spring a call and tell her you picked up the photograph she wanted, and you'll drop it off on your way home."

I'm sitting here at Check Out sweating it out.

I don't know whether Mrs. Timberlake believes my story about Lester Quinn's photograph or not. I suspect not. I suspect she's looking for retaliation for the remark about my mother and our chauffeur, grasping at straws, hoping she'll find something to hang me with.

Miss Spring is at the doctor's and can't be reached. Every two seconds, it seems like, though I know it's longer, Mrs. Timberlake toddles down and dials Miss Spring's number again.

I'll probably get written up as Suzy Slade, age fifteen, raiding the P-U.

They put everything in the newspaper out here. Even my mother was a DWI once, which means Driving While Intoxicated. She wasn't drunk, although the day the police-

38

man stopped her for driving over the yellow line she'd had a lot to drink, at lunch, at Tout Va Bien.

She said she deserved to be listed as a DWI, that it was a just punishment to put it in the newspaper for all to see. No one, said my mother, should drive a car if they can't stay on one side of the yellow line. But she was really mad about the fact they published her exact age, too.

"*That* I didn't deserve," she said. "It's bad enough for them to print that you're drunk when you're tipsy, but that you're age forty-six and you're drunk is damn cruel."

Naturally Nan got out of all of this. She's back there in the reading room humming around and straightening magazines.

When I finally called my father, he sounded as though I'd just awakened him. Don't ask me what that means: Daddy asleep in the middle of a beautiful May afternoon anyone else would give the shirt off his back to be out walking along the ocean in.

Daddy is not a nap taker, either.

He wants me to meet him right after I leave the library. We'll have an early dinner at Seaville Manor.

He's already okayed it with my mother.

Something's up, isn't it?

Five

"Is it okay if we eat dinner here, Suzy?" My father swallowed down the rest of his Scotch, and strapped a digital watch to his wrist.

"I've never had dinner here," I said. "Isn't this place a motel?"

"They serve very good meals in the coffee shop."

"It doesn't matter to me," I said.

"If you'd rather go someplace else—" he hesitated half-heartedly.

"What difference does it make?" I said.

He slipped into his tweed jacket, didn't bother with a tie, and slapped something sweet-smelling on his cheeks from a leather-bound jar on the bureau. Muzak was offering a syrupy version of "Fly Me to the Moon."

"Okay?" My father looked across the room at me. Then he opened the door, held it for me, and sang a few bars along with the violins.

" . . . In oth-ther words, hold me tight, in oth-ther words, dar-ling, kiss me."

I said, "You sound happy."

"Exceedingly so," he said.

"How come you're staying here and not at the house?"

"I don't get any work done at the house, and I've got a lot of work along with me."

It was a crummy coffee shop with a bar with gold wall-to-wall carpeting, gold paper place mats, and gold paper napkins. The walls were decorated with the kind of oil paintings they sell by the carload in supermarkets, and none of the flowers or plants were real. There was a gold rope separating the bar and dining room from the counter.

Daddy ordered a Chivas Regal and water for himself, a Coke for me, and the menu immediately.

I got the message: he wasn't in the mood for a leisurely dinner.

Almost before I got the words, "A hot turkey dinner with mashed and corn," out of my mouth, it was in front of me. Across from me Daddy began tearing away at a thick club steak, ordering another Chivas Regal and water for himself.

We made polite conversation until he got the second Chivas Regal down.

Then he said, "How do you feel about coming to live with me, Suzy?"

"How do *you* feel about it?"

"I'd be delighted to have you."

"That word again."

"What word?"

"Delighted. That's one of Mother's phoniest words."

"If you don't want to come and live with me," he said, "I certainly don't intend to force you. Your mother would be delight—" He stopped in the middle of the word and made a correction. "—your mother would love having both of you kids."

"You don't want either of us, do you?" I said it very calmly, almost as calmly as it came to me that he didn't. He really didn't. Here I was building up this big fear of being the one to leave Daddy by himself, if Chicago wouldn't change her mind, and the truth was *he* wanted out.

Daddy is the kind of man who would look like a dad if Hollywood were casting fathers. He's tall, black-haired, and broad-shouldered and very green-eyed. He's graying at the temples, skinny, and a pipe smoker. He throws his head back when he laughs, and has perfect white, straight teeth. When he's very serious he leans toward you and tries for a lot of eye contact.

He was trying for eye contact while I was staring down at my plate, smearing cranberry sauce all over my turkey.

"I love you. I love Chicago. I love you both very much," he said.

There was something really tacky about the situation. My father could afford to drive me down to Tout Va Bien, overlooking the ocean, where real violins play and the whole menu is in French. He could afford to make it a really beautiful evening, wherever it was leading. But there we sat in that nothing coffee shop eating slop that was more worthy of the Seaville High School cafeteria around Thanksgiving. And he was trying for eye contact and telling me he loved me.

Do you know something else? ESP, second sight, something like it told me that at that moment he was going to look at his watch. He did.

I said, "Wouldn't it be easier for you to just say what you have to say, Daddy?"

"I'm not going to force you to live in New York with me, Suzy."

"Fine," I said. I felt like crying, but I thought of people starving and losing loved ones in disasters, and I thought of little animals that were being cruelly experimented on in labs right at that moment—anything to keep me from self-pity. It worked. There were no tears.

In all honesty, why should I have cried? I didn't want to go to New York to live. All I wanted was for him to want me to go there and live with him.

"Oh, Suzy," he said, and he reached out to touch my hand.

I put my hand in my lap. "Daddy," I said, "it's all right. I didn't want to live in New York in the ninth place."

I sounded really neat. Mature. Cool. But not unwarm to him, not mean or pouty.

"You were always my big girl," he said. "I could always count on you."

I noticed his use of the past tense, as though something had come to an end.

"What's going on with you and Chicago?" I changed the subject.

"I don't think it's fair to discuss your sister behind her back."

"I'm just curious. . . . Why the motorcycle suddenly?"

"I was going to give her a car. She didn't want one. This boy—McKay was his name—he convinced her cars were trappings of the rich and privileged." Daddy chuckled.

"Scott Mckay," I said, suddenly pulling the name from my memory miraculously. "Chicago told me all about him."

Daddy frowned. "You see, Suzy, Chicago and I have been going through changes. I've changed. She's changed." He stopped for a moment, taking great care with what he planned to say. He was no longer the old daddy who couldn't mention Chicago's very name without being unable to suppress a silly grin. He said, "Maybe I've disappointed her."

"How?" I said. I wanted to help him say it right, if I could, whatever it was he seemed to want to say.

But he only shrugged and mumbled, "I don't know." I could tell he was planning to skip by any real reasons. He said, "Scott McKay was this wild kid Chicago took up with."

"A revolutionary," I said. "Chicago said he was an anarchist."

"A *kid*," Daddy said. "He was a kid. He began to change her ideas about things."

"She's changed a lot, too!" I said.

Daddy looked irritated. "She hasn't changed that much.

44

She wants fast things. A speedboat. She wants a speedboat for her birthday." He sighed. "A motorcycle. A speedboat."

"You're going to miss her, aren't you?" I tried to read in his eyes what he was feeling. I couldn't tell.

"I'll miss her. Yes."

"Don't worry about it," I reassured him. "We're actually sharing a bedroom."

"You're a good person, Suzy. I like you, as well as love you."

There was another glance at his watch.

I said that I didn't feel like having any dessert, even though I felt like something sweet, a hot fudge sundae to take away the floury taste of the turkey gravy. He didn't give me any argument. It was still light out as Daddy walked across to the parking lot where a cab was sitting.

"We're in luck. Your own private chauffeur at your service," he said.

"Fantastic!" I answered.

Then I turned around and looked up at him. "Daddy? We're all right, aren't we?"

"What do you mean, Suzy?"

"I mean you didn't lose your money or something awful like that?" I realized how ridiculous that sounded, as though that could be the worst thing to happen, and I half-expected Daddy to laugh at me and say something like, "Well, that wouldn't be the end of the world, would it?" but he didn't laugh. He just looked tired and almost like *he* was thinking of people starving and losing loved ones in disasters, thinking of little animals being experimented on in labs, to keep from feeling sorry for himself and crying. He hugged me to him hard for a moment and then he held me away, looking into my eyes. "I didn't lose my money, honey. There's nothing really wrong. I love you, Suz."

"Love you, too."

"I'll see you soon."

"Am I supposed to come in next weekend?"

"Was that when we had our date?"

"It doesn't matter," I said, realizing he'd forgotten the invitation.

"What do you mean, it doesn't matter? You better show up." He was making a gallant effort to sound enthusiastic.

"There are the Memorial Day games, anyway."

"Come the following weekend," he said.

I nodded.

"Okay?" he said. "Good!"

I didn't feel like going home, so I gave the taxi driver Miss Gwendolyn Spring's address.

She lives in a small apartment over a store called Coffee Beings. In addition to selling anything to do with coffee, the owners are always brewing various kinds they fresh grind, so Miss Spring's apartment usually smells great.

She was sipping a cold drink called a zombie, which she said she and Lester Quinn drank all through World War II, whenever they were together.

46

She made a lemonade for me, and listened while I told her all that had gone on at the library that afternoon. I told her how I felt about the Fabrizio, too; she was one of the few people I could tell.

She was wearing these red shorts with white socks and red sneakers, and a white T-shirt that said Phillips Air Force Base across it.

"You made a bad mistake," she said when she finished hearing me out, "by leaving Lester Quinn's photograph there when you went off for dinner with your father. If it was so urgent that you have it, you'd have remembered it. You're that way."

"I thought of that. I could claim my father's visit rattled me."

"I said it for you, Mama-doodle," she told me.

"Mrs. Timberlake doesn't know it was all a lie?"

"She doesn't know. I figured you were up in my office trying to see what you could see, and you got caught and made up that story. Well, it was a good story. If I *had* been sick, I *would* have felt better having Lester Quinn's photo with me."

"You weren't sick?"

"I went to a christening."

"Couldn't you get time off for that from Mrs. Timberlake?"

"Oh, I love these zombies," said Miss Spring sinking down into a rocker, and snapping on the record player. "I went to a christening for Davida Dix. I didn't think that would sit well with Mrs. Timberlake."

For a moment I didn't know why that wouldn't have sat well with Mrs. Timberlake, and then while Miss Spring continued, it came to me who Davida Dix was.

Miss Spring said, "It's hard for me to believe Lionel is a father. He's been coming into the library since he was a little tyke, taking out every book he could carry, reading who knows how many a week."

Davida Dix was Kelly Plante and Lionel Dix's new baby.

I didn't believe my own ears when I blurted out, "What color is the baby?"

I felt a blush spread across my face. I felt too ashamed to look Miss Spring in the eye.

She said, "The baby is very dark, like Lionel."

"I hate myself for asking," I said.

"Why do you hate yourself for asking? It's a normal question. It's not wrong to ask what color eyes a child has if his daddy's got brown ones and his mother's got green."

"That's a little different," I said.

"It shouldn't be. Lord, when will the world leave people alone, let people do what they want to do if they're not hurting other people!"

"I guess some people think a marriage like that isn't fair to the baby?"

"If we had to worry about what marriages were fair to the baby, we'd have a sudden decline in the population," said Miss Spring.

"But mightn't a mulatto have a hard time?"

"Who has an easy time? Are you having an easy time?"

I didn't answer her because a record called "I'll Never Smile Again," came over the speaker, and Miss Spring put her finger to her lips and said, "Shhhhhhhh. This was a favorite of Lester Quinn's and mine."

Before I left Miss Spring's, she said, "I'm glad you realize the Fabrizio is beautiful. 'Wild nights! Wild nights! Were I with thee!'" She gave a wistful chuckle and said, "I hope someday you realize how those words can hurt and pull and fill you."

"I wish I could write anything so beautiful as that poem."

Miss Spring put her finger up to my chin. "No, Mama-doodle. Wrong wish. Wish instead that you could *feel* anything so beautiful as that poem."

"Well, you have to feel it to write it."

"I don't think anyone who feels it could put it into words," said Miss Spring. "It has to be vicarious."

Then she said, "Good night, Mama-doodle. Rush straight home," and she did a sort of turn around the room, sweeping her arm down as though she were raising her skirts in a dance.

I went away hoping someday to taste a zombie, too.

When I got home, I wanted to call Nan to tell her Miss Spring had lied for me.

I went into the living room and picked up the phone.

In the saddest tone of voice I'd ever heard my father use, I heard him say, "Do you understand, Evelyn? I wish I could just get out of it, escape it, go to Mexico or some damn place and become a missing person."

There was a pause, quite a long one for my mother. Then she said, in an equally melancholy tone, "Oh, Barry, don't you realize that you already *are* a missing person?"

I hung up, not knowing what it was all about, afraid to listen anymore for fear of finding out.

Six

When I finally asked my mother what my father was going through, she said, "It was a great disappointment to me, Suzy, that you didn't hang up the phone the other night, when you heard your father and me talking."

"I did," I said, "eventually."

My mother can really make you sorry you asked a personal question by zinging you with something she's saved up especially for the occasion.

"Something's going on," I said, "and I'm curious."

"So was the Watergate crowd," said my mother, "and they didn't mind breaking the rules to satisfy their curiosity, either."

One of her tricky ways is to let me think that if I'd handled a situation in a quote/unquote grown-up manner, I'd have gotten much further with something I'd failed at. She pulled that on me where Daddy was concerned, pretending that because I'd listened in on their phone conversation, I'd spoiled my chances of learning something important which she was on the threshold of telling me.

Forget trying to reach Chicago, too. I would like to forget Chicago, period. She is trying to pole-vault with the boys' team at the Memorial Day games. No girl has ever done it before; no girl has ever wanted to. She is busy petitioning the principal and carrying around signatures of faculty and students who agree that she should be allowed to do it. If only it was not Chicago, my crazy sister in drag, I would have my own name on the petition, but I am already embarrassed enough by her. She is too different, too superoriginal for Seaville.

From what she tells me, she is a pretty good pole-vaulter, and the boys won't be sorry. Oceanside has better pole-vaulters than Seaville, and the competition on Memorial Day is sad when it comes to that sport in particular.

"With me, they could win," she told me while we were getting dressed Wednesday morning.

"With you they could lose face, too."

"They'll get over that after a while."

"Daddy left a message for you," I said, suddenly remembering something he'd told me at dinner. "Your speedboat will be at the Blue Marlin Marina in about a week. Your birthday present."

"Thanks a lot for telling me right away, Suzy," she said sarcastically.

"Your birthday isn't until next September," I shrugged.

(It has been four days since Daddy's visit.)

"I completely forgot to tell you," I said. "I wasn't being small."

"I'm dying to let that boat go in the bay," she said. "All the way."

"Another reason I didn't tell you before this is that you're never around much."

"I'm in school, every day, and you always rush off from me."

"I mean at night."

"I don't like hanging around this big house at night."

"Mother says you hang around the Hatefilled."

"Mother doesn't know where I hang around."

"Mother knows," I said. "She has Macaulay follow you in the Lincoln."

"The Hatefilled isn't even open yet."

"Mother says you lurk around there after dark and it gives her chills thinking about it."

"It's a good place to ride around there. She's the one who doesn't want me riding in town."

"Mother says," I continued, sounding like a parrot, "Macaulay says you don't ride much at all. He says you park your bike."

"Macaulay should leave spying up to the Pentagon."

I watched Chicago put on a bright-red silk shirt several sizes larger than she was.

"Is that a shirt of Daddy's?"

Chicago got this angry look on her face and suddenly let go for no reason I could figure.

"Suzy, did anyone ever tell you you're obsessed with Daddy? You can't settle on steady ground without knowing all about Daddy! You're like some cup hung up on a hook, you can't feel your feet! What's the matter with you, Suzy? Dad isn't the sun and the moon and the stars, he's just plain old Barry Slade, big businessman, son of an even bigger businessman, WASP, mortal, culpable, and all the other human adjectives that apply!"

I had a feeling she was lecturing herself.

"I don't care if you wear one of his shirts," I mumbled back. "I'm just surprised he'd pick out a shirt like that. Does he bowl in it or something?" (I already knew Daddy didn't bowl.)

Never mind what Chicago said Daddy did in that shirt; Chicago was in one of her really obscene tempers.

I listened to her while I finished hiding a pimple with Cover-It. The gist of her tirade seemed to be that she could do without Daddy, and every other Slade in the book.

She was never very eloquent, but since her return from New York she is a strong antonym to eloquent. Crude. As Martha Crammer would say, "Vulgar."

What doesn't begin with f begins with s, and it's as monotonous as Miss G. Spring always says petty sniping, petty snooping, and petty snubbing are. Miss Spring says someone who can deliver an insult with class can turn into an Oscar Wilde (Miss Spring's favorite dead playwright); someone who practices first-rate detecting can inspire a character like Sherlock Holmes, or intrigue a writer on the level of Josephine Tey (Miss Spring's favorite dead mystery writer); and someone who is talented at avoiding boring people can hostess a salon filled with celebrities, like Gertrude Stein (Miss Spring's favorite dead hostess of a salon).

It's never a particular action that's annoying, according to Miss Spring: it's the lack of vision, effort, and feeling that goes into it.

My sister's way of expressing herself lately does have feeling, anyway.

I didn't even want to watch Chicago get into the rest of her get-up. There was a pair of farmer's bib overalls in thin stripes, and boots that went to the knee and laced.

Maybe if some fashion editor threw them all together and got them on some model, pinning everything tightly so there was shape to the costume, and adding a dash with a scarf, some eye make-up, some gold accessories, it would have won a prize in Paris, and wound up being copied by Macy's. But on Chicago, these clothes just looked like more ugly drag.

The only thing that wasn't getting worse daily about

her was her hair. She was actually letting her hair grow.

I decided to go to school in a good mood and the heck with what was happening to Daddy or Chicago! It was such a beautiful May day, the kind of May day that reminds everyone of how great June is. Mother was off to some charity fair at a local church. She was tending an old-books booth in blue jeans and a big straw hat. Our gardener was out back fooling around with some new geraniums and azalea plants. Even Lena Klein was inspired to write a new poem, which we found out about after lunch.

Lunch was from 11:36 to 12:21. For a ninth grader, on a nice day, lunch means sitting on the front steps of school, or chancing ticks to sit out on the lawn and watch all the cars go by piled with sophomores, juniors, and seniors.

Martha Crammer sat with me, and we both moaned a lot about not knowing anyone with a car. Then Martha started talking about automobile accidents and what happens when you die (to make herself feel better about not knowing anyone with a car), and my good mood began to shrink to the size of a raisin.

At 12:25 I dragged myself down the hall to English, not even caring that at various points along the way there were huge signs pasted up saying:

SEAVILLE POLE-VAULTERS!

ANYTHING YOU CAN DO,
CHICAGO SLADE CAN DO BETTER!
ARE YOU AFRAID OF THE CHALLENGE?

Lena Klein's poem cheered up a lot of us, not just because she writes neat poems for a ninth grader, but also because of what she's like herself. She is a good friend of Nan Richmond's, and together they are a strange-looking pair. I think she could qualify for a legal albino, if there is such a thing. She has very white hair and pink skin, and these strange little weak eyes that dart around like a frightened rabbit's when she looks at you. But it is always Lena with her hand in the air, waving it wildly to read something she's written.

What I like about her is that she's this dippy-looking girl who really likes her own poetry, so somehow she becomes less and less dippy-looking in the face of her own confidence. She's so sure of herself when it comes to her own work, that you become unsure about your original judgment of the rest of her. You begin to think that for all you know people with white hair and pink skin and weak eyes that dart around like a rabbit's are rare beauties, and you've been freaking it for fifteen years without even realizing it.

This was Lena's poem, which she called

GLIMPSE OF LOVE
I saw them in front of someplace on the sand.
A man and his daughter, I surmised.
I saw him put her fingers one by one in his hand,
A man and his love, I realized.
I went past them staring.
Why?

Envying their sharing.
Why?
I shall never forget them by the sea,
Yet neither one of them even saw me.

I felt high again by the time I got to the library.

"Okay, Mama-doodle." Miss Spring seemed to be waiting for me as I came in the door. "Upstairs to my attic for a talk."

I glanced in Nan's direction but she shrugged her shoulders and looked away.

I followed Miss Spring, who was decked out in a black peasant skirt, white peasant blouse, and gray cardigan. Bobby socks as usual with saddle shoes. I breathed in the scent of Tweed as we went up the winding stairs.

She was huffing and puffing from the effort, and she was trying not to talk in a loud voice, which made her sound like someone with bad asthma.

"What right did you have to take personal property from the Seaville Free Library?"

"What?"

"And how *dare* *y*ou trespass on the Phineas Ulin collection!"

"Miss Spring," I said, "I didn't *take* anything. I told you about trespassing on the collection the other night at your house."

"You borrowed 'Wild Nights'!"

"No."

"You didn't borrow 'Wild Nights?'"

"Absolutely not."

"Then who did? That is the next question. Who did?"

I had never mentioned Nan's participation in our visit to the P-*U* collection.

"Do you have any idea who borrowed 'Wild Nights' for a night and then slipped it back here?"

"No," I said. "Are you sure about that?"

"I am positive, Mama-doodle!"

"I'm sorry I can't help you," I said.

"I trust you, you know," said Miss Spring.

I only nodded.

I didn't have to finish asking the question of Nan.

"I just wanted to show Roger," she said. "I wasn't going to make off with the valued treasure, or sell the rare erotica."

"You took it overnight?"

"I never thought she'd know."

"Miss Spring will get to the bottom of this if it kills her, Nan."

"It's just going to have to kill Owl Eyes, Suzy. I need my job. I can use my good reputation, too."

"Just as long as *I* don't get the blame," I said. "It can remain an eternal mystery."

"The Seaville Free Library Phineas Ulin Erotica Fabrizio 'Wild Nights' Mystery," Nan intoned. "And oh, Lordy, am I sorry I ever let that Roger look at it with his eyes!"

"What happened?"

58

"I could have been showing him the vestal of Christ—I don't know."

"What is the vestal of Christ?"

"I don't know what the vestal of Christ is, I made that up. What I mean is, I could have been showing him this holy something that changed his whole life and sent him crying into the wilderness."

"Nan," I said, "just tell me what happened."

"We had a major fight. I mean major. I dared to laugh in the wrong place or something. I dared to make light of the thing."

"Doesn't he know by now that things like that make you silly?"

"I don't know what he knows, but I do know I might have been laughing at the thorns in the crown or the nails in the cross."

"I like it myself," I said.

"*Like* it?" Nan was almost shouting. "He's all turned around, honey. His front's going backwards and his back's going toward the front. He also says everyone should be allowed to see its beauty. He says what kind of a *free* library locks such a thing up for the geriatric set to see and not those who can appreciate it!"

"He's got a point," I said. "Are you still fighting?"

"Does April come between March and May?"

"I'm sorry," I said.

"And now if Owl Eyes upstairs finds out and fires me, my goose is cooked every which way!"

"I like Miss Spring," I said. "Don't call her Owl Eyes."

I was feeling guilty for holding back information from Miss Spring, but I also wished Nan liked her better. I decided to tell her. "She went to the christening for Kelly and Lionel's baby, you know."

"No, I don't know, and if I did know, why should I give a damn?"

"Not a lot of people around here would do that," I said.

"Including yours truly," Nan said.

"Why not? I would have if Kelly'd asked me."

"I don't know Mrs. Kelly Plante Dix, but if she'd of asked me, honey, I'd of slapped her little white cheeks silly red, and then drawn blood from her two nostrils."

"She couldn't help falling in love with Lionel."

"And I can't help getting fed to my teeth with the honkies going after our men." She added a resounding Chicago-like expletive that I think Mrs. Timberlake heard and could not believe she heard.

Nan and I broke up as we saw her coming toward us, but not before Nan told me something.

Maybe it was something she would have told me all along. Maybe it was something she just got mad enough to tell me. I don't know.

What she said was that Lena Klein's poem was inspired by Lena seeing my dad with some young girl, on the beach, in front of Seaville Manor a few days ago.

Seven

Her name is Enid Rider and she is only two years older than Chicago. My father met her somewhere in the vicinity of Wall Street, where she was working as a cocktail waitress in a small restaurant.

"Does Mother know all about her, too?"

Chicago nodded. "Dad told her when he came out here."

We were standing in our bedroom. I was in pajamas, which I often put on right after dinner and wear through the evening. I wanted to sit down on the twin beds with her and really talk about it, but Chicago was in a mood to go somewhere on her Harley.

I was trying to make it less easy for her to do, by standing against the door.

Chicago had herself all dressed up in leather: black leather boots, black leather pants, black leather jacket, and a black leather cap. She was wearing the red silk shirt again, and she had a black scarf knotted around her neck.

She had a slightly ominous look, I thought, like she belonged to some gang. While she was struggling into the boots, I'd made some remark about wondering where the Hell's Angels were meeting. She'd answered that if she knew, she'd be the first one there, because their morals couldn't be any worse than those of the crowd on Ocean Road. I'd let the remark drop for a while, because I didn't want to get her angry before I found out as much as I could about Daddy's new girl friend.

I said, "I guess everyone knew about it but me."

"It's not something he's going around boasting about."

"Why did he bring her out here?"

"Because she doesn't let him out of her sight!" Chicago said.

"That doesn't sound like Daddy, letting a woman boss him around."

"You don't happen to *know* what sounds like Dad anymore, Suzy."

"Tell me then."

Chicago slapped a pair of leather gloves against her pants and gave a shrug of her shoulder. "He's gone around the bend. I think he'll probably marry her."

"*Daddy* will?" I couldn't help what came out of my mouth after Chicago's saying that.

But it made Chicago impatient with me. "Yes, Daddy will! %¢&*$*&! Suzy, you have got to take Dad down off that pedestal you have him on!"

"Me?" I said. "I hardly know Daddy. I don't really know him."

"Then stop saying what sounds like him and what doesn't. I know him, and I'm telling you he's hung by his eyeballs on this stupid little %678!!*&!"

"Poor Daddy," I couldn't help saying.

It infuriated Chicago. "Poor he isn't and decent he isn't and honest he isn't and he isn't any of the things little girls from rich families think their daddies are! Their daddies are crooks most of the time!"

"Daddy isn't," I said.

"He got rich at someone else's expense."

"Whose?"

"It's an expression, you dumb little #$!@#$!" Chicago said. "It's just an expression. It means that no one gets rich in this country unless someone else stays poor so he can get rich. A lot of someone elses, as a matter of fact."

I was thinking over what Chicago was saying, and remembering the earlier remark about the Hell's Angels and the people along Ocean Road.

I said, "Well, you sure don't mind *spending* his money!"

"Get out of the way, Suzy!" Her eyes were spitting fire, but I wanted to have my say, even if she did haul off and slug me. I always felt that someday violence could happen between us, fast and awfully.

I said, "You never worked for anything you have. In fact, you never worked."

"Oh, I suppose you call what you do at that &¢*%$& library work?"

"It's more than you ever did in your life, and yet you want the new motorcycle and the new boat and you moved back here on Ocean Road the minute things started getting the least bit rough on you in the city!"

"Move away from the door, Suzy!"

"Well, isn't what I just said true? And if Daddy is such a crook, what does that make you for wanting more and more all the time from him?"

I'd forgotten how strong my sister was. There wasn't any need for very much violence. One fast shove from her and I was sitting on my behind on the braided rug in our room. Chicago was out the door and down the stairs in a flash. I was still trying to digest all that had taken place between us when I heard the roar of her motor, and the kick of scattered gravel in the driveway as she took off.

I got up and went over to the window seat, staring out at the ocean for a while.

What bothered me most of all was the things I said to Chicago.

I know I should have been more bothered by this involvement of Daddy's with the nineteen-year-old girl. But I could only think how it must be hurting Chicago, and until that moment I hadn't realized how wounded she'd been when she'd come back to us.

She'd made all that up about Daddy's smothering her, and wanting to get out from under his thumb. What had really happened was that Daddy had found someone to take her place; Chicago was no longer number one in Daddy's life.

It also dawned on me that it wasn't just fast things Chicago was interested in lately—it was ways of escape. She was asking our dad to give her the means to get away: a motorcycle, a boat, some way out.

I began to worry at that point, and to dress at the same time.

It was just beginning to get dark out, and the only way I was going to see walking down Ocean Road was to take a flashlight. The Hadefield was a good mile from our house. It was the only place I could think to look for Chicago.

My mother was in the solarium watching television. The maids were in the kitchen eating dinner with the cook. It was Macaulay's night off.

I'd put all the lights on in my room, turned on the TV, and shut the door. I hoped Mother would think I was in there, as usual, watching my television and studying.

You have to understand that I didn't think I was wrong about what I'd said to Chicago. If she didn't approve of the way Daddy was making his money, she shouldn't have been so eager to help him spend it. She wasn't going to get any points from me because she chose a motorcycle over an automobile, or because she ran around in work-men's clothes, and talked tough out of the side of her mouth about Ocean Road people.

The thing was, I realized what made her feel so angry, and I felt suddenly so protective of her. I went stumbling down that dark road next to the ocean, appreciating for the first time in my life how much I loved Chicago.

It was nine thirty when I reached the Hadefield. The sky was pitch-black except for stars and a very thin slice of moon.

Perspiration soaked my jeans and my long-sleeved cotton shirt, and my feet hurt from half-walking, half-running.

Something told me I might be too late, that whatever it was which had made me race there, would now have already happened.

The place was dark, and I was beginning to believe it was not even where Chicago had headed for, when I saw the cycle.

I went past it, up over a dune, calling Chicago's name.

My flashlight in that foggy ocean darkness was of no more use than a kitchen match.

"Chicago?" I called. "Chicago?"

There was no sound but the surf slapping the beach. I could feel the dampness get into my hair, and a chill swept through me. I didn't know if I was cold or afraid. Both, probably.

Then I saw a very small light coming from inside the Hadefield. It was a flickering light. Someone was in there, with a fire going in the fireplace.

I ran as well as you can on sand. I didn't have any breath left to call her name. Anyway, it had to be her in there—I was sure.

By the time I reached the deck of the Hadefield, I think I knew my sister wasn't there alone. I might even have seen something through the window, looked in and seen them there before the fire. I don't know. I can't remember.

I do know I knocked on the door, and I waited for someone to come, so I must have known, seen, sensed something.

My sister didn't answer my knock. He did.

I could see my sister beyond him, sitting in front of the fire with her knees pulled up, hugging her knees with her arms, sitting in profile, not facing the door or paying attention to what was going on, until she heard me say, "Hello, Roger."

Eight

"I love athletes," Lena Klein said as she and Nan and I walked to the Memorial Day games, "but I've never been able to write a poem to one."

"It's a good thing," Nan said. "Except for Roger, most of them can hardly string a sentence together, much less read a poem. Particularly the honkies."

"But that isn't why," said Lena, brushing back a wisp of white hair from her squinty eyes. "The reason I've never been able to write a poem to one is I've never seen the male body. I think that hinders me."

I'd been halfway into my own head before that statement. I was wondering again if Nan had noticed anything different about Roger. Every day I waited with dread for that to be the day Nan found out.

"You've never seen *any* male body?" Nan was flabbergasted.

So was I. "Not even pictures?" I said.

Lena shook her head. "You have a brother, Nan. I'm an only child."

"Still and all, baby," said Nan, "we are emerged from the dark ages into the light ages, you along with us! I don't believe my own big ears!"

"Of course A.E. Housman wrote a perfectly beautiful poem about an athlete without mentioning anything about his body, but I'm more tactile."

"Oh, you're more tactile!" Nan mocked her, and I could tell Nan wasn't sure what tactile meant. "You're more stupido, as they say down Mexico way. Anyone who wants to see a male body can see a male body in this day and age."

" 'To-day, the road all runners come, Shoulder-high we bring you home,' " Lena recited. "That's Housman's 'To an Athlete Dying Young.' "

Nan nudged my ribs with her elbow. "We ought to show her 'Wild Nights' sometime." She said to Lena, "It's a Fabrizio."

I said in a whispered aside to Nan, "It wouldn't surprise me if Miss Spring hired a detective to solve the Seaville Free Library Phineas Ulin Erotica Fabrizio 'Wild Nights' Mystery."

"She's still harping on it and Roger's still harping on it," said Nan.

"I always regret that Fabrizio died before he could illustrate one of my poems," Lena said wistfully.

"What do you mean, Roger's still harping on it?" I asked Nan.

"He says I don't have any soul."

" 'Speed the soft intercourse from soul to soul, And waft a sigh from Indus to the Pole,' " Lena recited. "That's from Pope's 'Eloisa to Abelard.' "

Nan told her, "You got intercourse and male bodies on the brain, Lena Klein."

I asked Nan, "Is everything okay between you and Roger?"

"Sure," Nan said, "except for his new job. I never see him anymore."

"What kind of a job?" I felt like a traitor, playing dumb that way.

"Guarding the Hadefield until it opens. He sleeps there."

"That poem has nothing to do with *sexual* intercourse, Nan. You're the stupido," said Lena.

Nan said, "When I do see him, he gives lectures. The Seaville Free Library isn't really free like it claims, because people have to pay for library cards, and there's a pay duplicate section, and the P-*U* collection isn't available to the general public. He's come down with radicalitis since he's been guarding the wealth over in the Hadefield."

"I'd personally love to see the Fabrizios myself," said Lena.

Nan said, "Today's going to be the first day I'm going to see him in a long time, and look at all the people I got to share him with!"

The Memorial Day games are a big event in Seaville. Everyone anywhere near the town comes in to watch them. Even some of the weekend tourists attend if the weather is too cloudy for the beach.

This Memorial Day it was sunny and cool. All the downtown streets were filled with people trooping toward the Crammer Memorial Stadium. The traffic was thick, and there was a real air of festivity in Seaville.

The town drunk was near the entrance of the stadium, very drunk, what my mother calls "bouncing-off-walls drunk." He was shouting at the top of his lungs that the only sport that wasn't fixed was the rodeo.

Nan and I smiled as we walked by. Lena looked away. A lot of townspeople looked away when they saw him, but Nan and I felt like we knew him really well, because he was in the library so often.

"You can't bribe the bulls and the horses, can you, girls?" he said. Then he slammed into a brick wall and cracked his head so hard I heard it, and felt for him with a chill down my own spine. I felt so sorry for him. It made me remember something Chicago had said to me one morning when we were both getting ready to leave the house.

"When I was very young I felt sorry for people, and I might again when I'm very old, but right now there's not room for that."

"I still feel sorry for Daddy," I had insisted. Chicago had refused another phone call from him which came while we were all eating breakfast. Even Mother had given Chicago her most imploring look, but Chicago just shook her head no. Then I had had to get on the phone, Old Second Choice, and Daddy tried to sound really enthusiastic about my coming into New York the next weekend for a visit.

"I know you feel sorry for him," said Chicago. "That's your privilege. Remember what I told you the other night, Suzy: I'll never interfere with you, and don't you ever interfere with me."

"Is asking questions about your relationship interference?"

She'd intimidated me so I was even afraid to say Roger's name. I said "your relationship," or "your situation."

That night when I found them together at the Hadefield, Roger had been ready to ask me into the clubhouse. "Have some fire, little live wire," and he'd given me his big wide white smile. But Chicago was on her feet in seconds, and she wasn't about to welcome me in. She told me to hightail it back home fast, and if there was anything to discuss, we'd discuss it the next day.

The next day she said, "Keep your mouth shut about last night and we'll get along fine."

I just shrugged.

Then she sort of touched my hand, the back of it, with a gentle tap of her fist. "Don't worry about it, Suzy. Okay?"

I said, "Sure. But I hope you know what you're—"

Her fist opened and her palm came up to cover my mouth, not in a rough way. "Hush, Suzy. Just hush!" she said emphatically.

I've been hushed on that subject ever since then, until I'd asked her if asking questions was interference.

She answered, "The worst kind."

"Then forget it," I said.

She said, "Suzy?"

"What?"

"It hasn't got anything to do with Dad."

"Who said it did?" I said.

"No one," she answered.

One thing: ever since that night Chicago's been different with me. She hasn't been flying into those rages, and she hasn't been cussing the way she did before. I don't know if it has to do with something between her and me, or between them. I don't know what's softened her, but she's softened.

Nan was right about sharing Roger with everyone, because Roger was winning a lot.

It seemed like every two seconds over the loudspeaker, we heard Roger's name ring through the stadium.

He wrestled and pinned his opponent in seventeen seconds, in the 177-pound weight bracket.

He vaulted eight feet nine inches, and won that event. (Chicago had lost her battle to vault. I often think the whole thing between Roger and her must have begun when she was fighting to participate in that event. I wonder why I care so much when it began. I do. I try to picture what took place before I found them that night in front of the fire. Was that the reason Chicago was letting her hair grow? It was his red silk shirt, wasn't it? I go over things in my mind, trying to visualize things and reconstruct them.)

Roger won the mile race, was second place in the discus, and third in the hammer.

He even won the prize for the largest chest: "Roger Coe III, the winner!" the announcer shouted, "Thirty-nine inches!"

Nan was rollicking in and out of fits of laughter, applauding and calling out, "Oh honey! Oh hon-*ney*!"

My eyes were searching the rows of seats for some sign of Chicago. I couldn't spot her. I didn't even know where to look. She didn't have any friends. My mother hadn't come this year. She was over on the North Shore at a fund-raising plant sale. Where would my sister even be if she was there? Not with Roger's family, certainly. I saw them. They were all gathered down toward the front. Old Roger the First, B.C., who was supposed to be the best gardener in Hammock County; then Jr., Roger's father, who ran a soul-food place in Inscape; his mother, who was carrying a new little brother; and the other brothers, five of them. I remember Nan saying Roger liked to brag that the only female Coes were the ones the males married.

After all the prizes were announced, everyone started spilling onto the field while the Seaville High band played. Lena and I talked about walking into Patches for some pizza, but Nan said she was going to wait for Roger.

"He'll be coming up here to find me."

"Did he say so?" I asked.

She gave me this look of disbelief.

"Okay," I said. "I just wondered."

We left her there, sitting in the sun, listening to some music over the small transistor Roger had given her, which she always carried.

Lena was saying, "I think it would disillusion me to see the male body, anyway."

"Probably," I said.

We were walking toward the exit, past the turn to the locker rooms. Then I saw Chicago. She was wearing her crash helmet and sitting just outside the men's locker room, with her motor warming. You couldn't tell whether it was a boy or a girl, unless you knew Chicago.

Lena said, "We better hurry if we don't want to wait in line."

"Okay," I said. Then I said, "Was the girl with my father at least pretty?"

"She was a redhead," Lena said. "I noticed that right

74

away because they were lying on the blanket together in this brilliant sun. I have skin as sensitive as a redhead's, if not more sensitive. So I was thinking to myself, How can she take the sun with skin like that?"

"My father might marry her is why I asked," I said.

"My mother said he won't. She said Barry Slade is too smart a man to walk into that kind of a trap!"

"What kind of trap?" I asked.

"Some kind of trap about a wife becoming a legal heir," said Lena, brushing back another wisp of white hair, and blinking up at me with her little pink eyes. "I'm sorry, Suzy."

My shoulders were getting all kinds of exercise, because all I was doing lately was shrugging.

" 'I know,' " Lena began reciting, " 'that we can never be friends after, never hear each other's laughter, after it is finished, *we* will be.' "

"Who wrote that?" I asked.

"I did," she said. "I took the liberty of writing about the end of your father's affair."

I didn't say anything. We went and stood in line for pizza and watched the sophomores, juniors, and seniors take off in cars for McDonald's, and the Big Steer, roaring down the street, screaming with happiness.

Pretty soon I saw Nan heading our way alone. She had a puzzled look on her face. It wasn't a look of anger, nor even one of doubt, just this look of surprise, as though there had been some terrible mistake.

75

Chicago didn't show up for dinner that night. My mother said she could hardly blame her. It was a beautiful day, and Chicago's XK-18 jet Chris Craft had been delivered early to the Blue Marlin Marina.

"She's probably taking someone for a ride," my mother said.

Nine

"Have a delightful time, honey," my mother said as she let me off at the train station the next weekend, "and tell your father Chicago sends love."

"He'll know that's a lie," I said. "Chicago won't even talk to him on the telephone."

"He might want to believe it hard enough not to care that it's a lie," my mother said. "Try it, Suzy! Here comes your train!"

I swung my knapsack over my shoulder and found myself running alongside Gwendolyn Spring. I was glad to see her, since she'd been distant after the Fabrizio incident.

"Are you going to New York?" I asked.

"Only to Oceanside, Mama-doodle. I've got some shopping to do."

I was surprised, because Saturday is one of the busiest

days at the library. It is also the one day in the week people from out of town call to see the P-*U* collection.

"You sit by the window," she said. "I hate looking out of train windows and being seen by people staring at me from someplace. It's like having them watch me go while they stay. Maybe the war did that to me. I saw him off on so many trains and felt so sorry for him. He never liked travel, never went anywhere that he could help it, not even for a Sunday drive."

I never have to ask who "he" is.

I said, "I look at it in another way, that I'm going someplace and the people staring at me are standing still."

"Motion isn't necessarily going someplace, Mamadoodle," she advised. "Anyway, if he's bothering to come all the way here, it must be something very important. Earthshaking, to make Lester Quinn get on a train."

"What are you talking about, Miss Spring?"

"Haven't you heard? Everybody else has!"

She was like my mother in that way. My mother always said this and that was "all over town," which meant about twelve people in Seaville knew whatever it was. When Miss Spring said "everybody," it meant the employees of the Seaville Free Library, period.

"Is Lester Quinn coming to Seaville?" I asked.

"You guessed it, Mama-doodle. I'm on my way to Oceanside to shop for something to wear."

"Why's he coming?"

"That is the question. *That* is the big question of the day."

"Did he just call you and tell you he was heading this way?"

"I wonder if I can trust you."

"What?"

"I wonder if I can trust you," Miss Spring said, already digging into her bag, "with his personal letter to me. Suzy, if you're going to blab the contents all over Seaville so that any shred of intimacy between Lester Quinn and me is destroyed, then don't reach out for this."

She handed me the letter.

"I won't tell anyone," I said, and I hoped with all my heart that I meant it. Because I have gone back on my word, in some cases; sometimes I've come close to bursting trying to keep a secret, and then blurted it out and felt both better and just awful at the same time.

The letter was written in a very tiny script. It was short.

Dear Gwen,

I would like to come to see you on a personal matter which I know sounds funny since there has been nothing personal between us for so long now.

If there is someone in your life and you are too busy I would understand as after all I didn't expect you to be the famous one-man woman of legend.

Otherwise I will come next Monday and call you at the library—if you still work there—when I get in.

Yours,
Les

"Neat!" I said. "Real neat!"

"Oh, honey, learn to express yourself in a way appropriate to the situation. It is not 'neat' that Lester Quinn is making a reappearance in my life; it is magical, enchanting, something grand and predestined."

"You're right," I said. "Neat is a dumb word and I say it for everything lately."

"You'll grow out of it, Mama-doodle." She smiled up at me and pushed the letter back into her purse. She crossed her little legs and swung them in the manner of a child anticipating something happy. Then she took off her Coke-bottle-bottom glasses and blew on them to clean them. Without them she had these lovely wistful gray-changing-green shaded eyes, and as she jumped about, her blond curls bobbed. She couldn't keep from smiling.

She said, "Little does he know how much I have always been the 'famous one-man woman of legend.' Right down to the traditional evening zombies he loved so in the war. We drank them and listened to the records of Harry James and Tommy Dorsey and Glenn Miller. I remember in particular a favorite called 'Speak Low.' 'Speak low, when you speak love,' it went, though I can't remember any more and I don't even recall the band or the singer or much more than that we used to hold hands, my one finger rubbing his big red-stoned ring, drinking zombies and feeling so full of one another."

"How come Mrs. Timberlake let you have Saturday off?" I said.

79

"Suzy, you have a very practical nature. There's nothing wrong with a practical nature, but it always comes as a blow to one with a more romantic side. I tell you of a very priceless time, and you ask me how Mrs. Timberlake let me have Saturday off. . . . I *told* her I was taking it off."

I said, "Oh."

"You just tell someone when you have to. You rise to the occasion."

"Didn't she ask you why?"

"I told her why."

"Wasn't she surprised?"

"Honey, I don't think anyone is really going to be surprised. Not really in their heart of hearts. I have been anticipating this for as long as I have been without him. Haven't I?"

"Yes, ma'am."

"Do I look like someone loose from the loony bin?"

"No, ma'am," I said. She was wearing her hair pinned in bobby pins with a bandana over her head, a peasant skirt (as she called it), and a sheer white blouse and espadrilles.

"Therefore there had to be a semblance of reason to my waiting, a seed of truth to my trust. Fiber to my faith."

"I'm glad, ma'am," I said.

"Oh, so am I, Suzy. So am I!"

In a way, I wasn't glad. The first thing that had popped into my head when I saw her running alongside me for the train was that I might finally be able to talk with someone about Chicago and Roger. Miss Spring was so understanding where Kelly Plante and Lionel Dix were concerned, I thought she might tell me something to make me feel Chicago wasn't doing something wrong.

(Don't misunderstand me and think the "wrong" I worried about was the fact Chicago is white and Roger black—that worried me, it did, and there's no saying it didn't—but what I thought was "wrong" was what Nan had said about white girls going after the black boys.

Nan said it never worked the other way around, because in high school it was always the male athletes the fuss was over. The males were always the stars.)

I decided to take a stab at getting Miss Spring's mind off Lester Quinn, anyway, and I said, "Miss Spring, Nan says Kelly Plante had no right to Lionel Dix. She says Kelly should have stuck to her own kind."

"Is that all you and Nan Richmond have to talk about, honey? There you are, surrounded daily by the great and beautiful ideas of the world, and all you and Nan have to do is dish Kelly and Lionel?"

"We discuss other things, too."

"I should hope so. Now. To answer your question, even though it wasn't framed as a question: in my opinion, what talking about can stop, never started. Do you understand?"

"Sort of."

"What Nan says, what you say, what Martha Crammer says, what anyone in Seaville says, isn't going to change the way Kelly and Lionel feel, so Kelly and Lionel must be a unit, a couple, and their own kind . . . what some might call a blend, but very definitely two as one."

"Wouldn't it make you mad, though, if you were a black girl, seeing white girls go after your men?"

Miss Spring said quickly and flatly, "Yes."

I sighed heavily and stared out the window at the beginnings of summer evident everywhere, all new and green. I wondered how long the thing between Chicago and Roger would stay new, and where it would lead.

Miss Spring touched the back of my hand with a press of her fingers. "Life isn't answers, Mama-doodle," she said. "It's questions."

"I just wonder if there's ever really such a thing as right or wrong?"

"I can't remember who said it, honey, but someone said that right is what you feel good after, and wrong is what you feel bad after."

Then she turned and looked at me in that certain searching way of hers. She said, "Suzy? Do you remember the story *Member of the Wedding*. It's by Carson McCullers?"

I shook my head no.

"Well, you read it sometime. It's all about a young girl getting caught up in her brother's wedding, so caught up in it she was losing her own identity. You read it," she said again.

"I'm not losing my identity," I said, "though sometimes I think I wouldn't mind if I was."

"You just let Nan Richmond and Roger Coe live their

82

lives, and you start concentrating on your own."

I'd gotten her off on the wrong track and there was no way I was going to get her on the right one, unless I told her about Chicago and Roger. I couldn't do it, so I just shrugged and shut up about that particular subject.

Miss Spring's last words on the matter were, "When you do fall in love, Suzy, I hope it will make a bigger person out of you than it's made out of Nan. Why should Nan be so bitter about so many things when she's got a fine young man like Roger?"

I wanted to say, Maybe she can't believe it's true, because some part of her senses that it isn't.

"I could forgive anyone anything," said Miss Spring, "now that Lester Quinn is back in my life."

After she got off at Oceanside, I tried to stop thinking about Chicago and Roger. Maybe I *was* losing my identity; maybe what I ought to worry about, I decided, was where *I* was heading. What did I want to be, and who did I want to be it with? Both questions began to depress me and I wondered if I ought to have gone to that shrink. My mother said I could. That was just after the divorce, when my mother was trying to gauge my reactions to not having Daddy around.

Maybe I should have stretched out on his couch and told him pointblank, "The trouble is, I wonder if I really feel something, or if I imagine that I feel something. And if I *really* feel things, why am I always wondering if this is the way things really feel?"

I saw him in my mind's eye saying, "You are too sick for words," and then he would push a button and I would disappear, couch and all, into thin air.

So much for thoughts while riding a train. I think train riding makes you a little crazy, unless you've brought along a book or a crossword puzzle. Just looking out the window at the countless other houses, other lives going by endlessly, makes you think, Where do I fit in the scheme of things? I'm just another stick of human being, like another stick of furniture in some mammoth warehouse on the outside of the city limits.

To all of this Evelyn In-Analysis-For-Eight-Years Slade would respond, "Really, Suzy, sort your thoughts out better before you express them. You sound neurotic, otherwise, and you know you're one Slade who isn't at all neurotic."

I sometimes suspect she thinks I'm too unexciting to be neurotic, and maybe I am.

None of the johns on the Long Island Rail Road ever work, so the first thing I did when we arrived at Penn Station was to hunt one down. I somehow managed accidentally to get into one of the large wash-up ones with a basin and a mirror.

It's hard to resist a mirror when you're feeling super-dramatic, so I spent a little time talking to my reflection, saying things like, That's okay, kid, *I* like you. Who needs the rest? We'll stick it out through thick and thin.

Then I had this fantasy that Enid Rider, my father's new whatever-you-want-to-call-it, asked me to be the one to tell him she just couldn't take it any longer, she'd left him.

"Look," I said, with a very sincere countenance, "you ought to be big enough to go to him and tell him that yourself."

She said back, "But, Suzy, I never was a big person, and I can't keep on with the act."

I told her, "Chicago's the only one who can handle this."

Then I washed my hands and dried them under the blower, and headed toward the taxi sign.

On the way down to 19th Street I worried that Daddy might even have forgotten I was coming. Maybe nobody'd answer the bell when I rang it.

I paid the driver and said, "What are my chances of being mugged in broad daylight while I wait to see if someone answers the door?"

"Am I a fortune teller?" he said. "Is this a taxicab or a gypsy tearoom?"

But he waited when I got out, until Daddy appeared in the doorway.

Daddy said, "Do you owe him something, honey?"

The cab took off before I could answer, and then I was dumbstruck when I looked down as Daddy took my bag from my hands. On the third finger of his left hand was a shiny new wedding ring.

Ten

When my father's nervous he clasps his hands together and cracks his knuckles. He was doing that as he led me down the long hallway of his apartment, toward the garden in the rear.

He didn't say anything.

I said, "Chicago sends her love," and he sort of grimaced and smiled at the same time.

I said, "It wasn't a bad trip, but the johns on the train didn't work."

Then straight ahead I saw this redheaded girl stretched out on a chaise in the sun. She had on a pair of enormous dark glasses with a bright-green tint, and a green floppy straw hat. She had on a bikini and she was sitting up as my father opened the screen door leading to the garden.

"Enid, honey, Suzy's here," said my father.

She sat up on the edge of the chaise, so that her feet were touching the grass. I noticed she had painted toenails, orange-colored ones, and as I glanced up from them I saw her holding out her hand for me to take.

I went across and shook her hand. She had a tight grip, but she let go fast. She took off her glasses and stared up at me with these enormous round brown eyes.

"Aren't you sweet, honey," she said. "Your daddy didn't tell me you'd look so sweet. I love your dress."

I didn't love my dress because I'd had a long argument with my mother about wearing it. I'd wanted to wear pants.

I didn't exactly warm up to her right away, either, because she wasn't that much older than I was, yet she was talking down to me.

I said, "How do you do," since I couldn't dream up anything snazzier under the circumstances, particularly as I noticed the two rings on the third finger of her left hand. One was this gold band with a circle of diamonds embedded in it. The other was this diamond about the size of a Midol tablet.

"Suzy," said my father, "we have a surprise."

"You're married."

"We were married yesterday. It wasn't much of a ceremony."

"You can say that again," said Enid. "But I told Barry-bones here that the only important thing is that we become Mr. and Mrs., and if it's not going to happen in St. Pat's on Fifth Avenue with a big whoop-de-doo at the St. Regis after, I could care less. Do you know what I mean, honey? It's not important to have all that fuss."

Behind her there was a small Yorkshire terrier smelling some geraniums planted in beds at the back of the garden. Enid clapped her hands and said, "Fancy, you come over here and meet your new sister."

87

Daddy laughed nervously.

"Now you come over here, Fancy, and meet Suzy," said Enid.

Daddy said, "How was your train ride?"

"It wasn't a bad trip but the johns on the train didn't work."

"Nothing works on the Long Island Rail Road," Daddy said.

Enid was holding Fancy up to my face. "Give Suzy a kiss, honey."

The dog lapped the air with its tongue.

"You got a nice sister. *Two* sisters," Enid said.

For no reason, I said again to Daddy, "Chicago sends her love."

"Now there's someone I personally find fascinating," said Enid. "Chicago."

I guess she realized how that sounded because she allowed no more than a second's pause before she jumped in with, "But you're going to be my favorite. I can just tell. Do you know how sometimes you can just tell about something like that right from the beginning?"

I couldn't think of anything to say to that.

Enid said, "You work at the library out in Seaville, your daddy tells me."

"Yes, ma'am," I said, feeling foolish calling her ma'am.

She began smearing herself with Bain de Soleil, rubbing it up and down her legs as she talked. She said, "I love to lose myself in other men's minds. When I am not walking,

88

I am reading. I cannot sit and think. Books think for me."

I wasn't sure I heard right. Daddy was busy making a big production out of taking a cigarette from his gold case, lighting it and inhaling.

I guess I said, "What?" because she suddenly repeated, word for word, "I love to lose myself in other men's minds. When I am not walking, I am reading. I cannot sit and think. Books think for me."

Daddy came to the rescue. "Enid's always got her nose in a book," he said.

Enid said, "I read *Time* magazine, *The New Yorker*, and *Vogue*, every week."

I didn't bother offering the information that *Vogue* was not a weekly but a monthly.

Daddy said, "Would you like to change to something more comfortable, honey? Then Mrs. Bowen will serve us lunch out here."

"I'll put my jeans on," I said.

Enid said, "Want one of my bathing suits, honey?"

She had to know I was not a five as she was, but a seven. I said, "Thanks, anyway. The sun isn't a big deal to me, since I live right on the ocean." I was being a little bitchy, like my mother could be at times.

"Barrybones and I are going to look for something right on the ocean, too, aren't we, lovey?"

"I guess so," said my father, and I knew it wasn't an idea he was too keen about from his tone of voice.

Then Daddy walked me back down the long hallway

and up the staircase to the second floor of the town house. "You remember where Chicago's room is, don't you?" he said.

I said, "Yes. . . . Does Mother know you married her?"

"I'm going to phone your mother later today."

"You did it kind of suddenly, huh?"

"It was in the wind," he said.

"What?"

"It was in the cards, Suzy," he said.

"I don't exactly know what that means," I said.

"It means I was planning to marry her."

"Oh."

"There wasn't any reason not to marry her."

"I'll change into my jeans," I said as we got to the doorway of Chicago's room.

"Mrs. Bowen will serve us lunch in the garden," my father said.

I noticed he hadn't asked me what I thought of Enid. I hadn't offered to say what I thought, either.

What I thought was: *Why?*

In great big neon-lighted capital letters—WHY?

I wasn't the only one who thought my dad was something special. It was all spelled out in any *Who's Who*, in write-ups in *Business Week, Fortune*; even *Sunday Interview* had televised half an hour on him.

What was someone like my daddy doing with *her?*

Marrying her?

I sat down on Chicago's bed and stared at a huge poster

of James Dean, this dead movie actor Chicago used to idolize. He had these beautiful sad eyes and this haunted face, and Chicago used to say it was an expression that almost seemed to say, I know I won't make it. I'd seen him once in a picture called *Rebel Without a Cause*, which Chicago had seen seven times, along with every film James Dean ever made. I think she really loved him, if that's possible. He died before she saw his first movie, but I think Chicago was in love with him at one time.

I looked at his face, and I remembered the way he and the actress Natalie Wood and the actor Sal Mineo all hid out in this castlelike place, in *Rebel Without a Cause*—three of them against the world, sort of. God, I could have used a couple of pals and a castle to hide out in right at that moment.

I sat on the bed and sighed a lot and said Daddy, Daddy, Daddy, over and over for a while, and then the old functional side put an end to the dramatics. I fished my jeans out of my knapsack, slipped a T-shirt over my head, pushed my feet into my sandals, and went downstairs for lunch.

For lunch we had avocado stuffed with lobster salad and iced tea. Daddy drank a couple of Chivas Regals with water on the side. Enid said she never drank and didn't like it when Barrybones had too much to drink. My father didn't bother to acknowledge the remark.

Then Enid said, "You'll learn something about me,

91

Suzy. I am the easiest person in the world to understand. I take good care of myself and don't allow myself to dissicate my strength."

"*Dissipate*," said my father.

"That's right. I don't allow myself to do that to my strength. Do you know, Suzy, that I am never lonely, never depressed, never jealous of what others have? I can find everything I want in Bonwit Teller's, never mind a three-hundred-and-ninety-five-dollar Adolfo, or a six-hundred-and-fifty-dollar Halston. I am perfectly content with off-the-rack."

I was having trouble thinking of things to say, so I decided to try the same thing she was dishing out. I said, "That's a really great bracelet you have there."

As a matter of fact, I did like the bracelet. It was a simple gold chain.

She looked down and pulled at it for a moment. "Oh, honey," she said, "this thing cost me four dollars and fifty cents in Mexico years ago. It's not worth anything, honey, but if you like it I'll take it up to Cartier and have it dipped in gold, and it's all yours."

"Don't do that," I said.

"Why not, honey? Why shouldn't I do that if you like it?"

"It's just a lot of trouble," I said.

"It wouldn't be any trouble. Barrybones, don't you let me forget to take this up to Cartier and have it dipped in gold for Suzy to have, okay?"

"Don't say things you're never going to do," my father said.

"I don't know what you mean by that, Barrybones," Enid said. She looked quite angry. She had stopped eating. Her fork was filled with lobster salad and she was waiting now for my father to answer her.

"Enid," my father said, "you're always saying you're going to have this thing fixed for this one, and that thing cleaned so you can give it to that one, and none of it ever happens."

"Don't you say that even in jest," said Enid, her brown eyes snapping furiously. "Barry Slade, don't you ever say that even in jest! My promise is golden, and don't you try to make it sound any other way!"

"Okay. Your promise is golden," my father relented.

"You bet your ass it is!" said Enid.

Then she suddenly put down her fork with the lobster salad still on it, pushed back her chair, and charged out of the garden, slamming the door after her.

My father had this simpering smile on his face. I don't know if it was a smile of embarrassment or a smile of Chivas Regal. It was probably a combination of both.

Later that afternoon while I was listening to tapes in the garden, the sounds of my father and Enid arguing wafted down from the third floor. I was only able to make out a few full sentences.

Enid said, "What were you trying to incinerate?"

"*Insinuate!*" my father corrected her. "Speak the English language!"

At another point in the battle, Enid said, "I could have married him and lived on his yacht, which is about the size of Denmark, in case you're not familiar with it!"

"He wouldn't have married *you*, baby. Don't kid yourself!" my father shouted back. "I'm the only jackass that would have *married* you."

I guess this went on for about an hour and a half. I heard something break (a vase? a picture frame?), and my father's language became really deletable.

After a while, I suddenly realized everything up on three was very quiet. I could see the wind blowing the curtain in a lazy breeze, and the shade of their room was pulled down three-quarters of the way.

I went into the house to get something cold from the kitchen, and I saw Fancy looking very lost and sad, peering out of a large green straw bag, which matched Enid's straw hat. It was in a corner of the living room.

"Are you locked out?" I asked Fancy. I went across and picked her up. As I lifted her out of the bag, I noticed a book inside. It was *The International Thesaurus of Quotations.*

There was a book of matches holding a place near the beginning of the thesaurus, and I opened it to that page.

Penciled in the margin were the words: "Memorize for Suzy's visit."

The page was 91; the heading was "Books and Reading."

94

Number 55 was outlined in red: " 'I love to lose myself in other men's minds. When I am not walking, I am reading. I cannot sit and think. Books think for me.' Charles Lamb. 'Detached Thoughts on Books and Reading.' *Last Essays of Elia* (1833)."

I knew then I could never really dislike her. I felt for her all the things she claimed she never dissipated her strength to feel. I felt lonely and depressed for her.

I picked up her little shivering Yorkie and hugged and stroked it.

I said, "Oh, Fancy, your mama named you that, didn't she?"

Fancy kept right on shivering, even though I held her securely and lovingly in my arms. It was as though nothing could ever make her feel really safe, and not anyone.

Eleven

That Saturday night Daddy took Enid and me to dinner at a rooftop restaurant. It was on the sixty-fifth floor of a building in New York City, and you should have been able to see the entire city from up there. But a combination of clouds and pollution gave everything a yellow, hazy look until it was very dark, and then it was just thick fog.

I was glad I'd brought a dress to New York with me, because Enid got herself up in this white Dior gown, and my father went along with the act and wore a black tie. I told them they could both claim they were treating this orphan girl to a big night in the city, if they wanted to pretend I wasn't theirs. My little green-and-white cotton number had come from the only seedy department store anywhere near Seaville. Mother doesn't believe in spending a lot on a wardrobe when one is still growing, and, as she's fond of pointing out, there's no one to hand things down to, as there was in Chicago's case. (You can imagine how much I enjoyed Chicago's hand-me-downs, too.)

Enid said I looked "sweet," which made me all the more uncomfortable, and "Anyway," said Enid, "I could care less about this Dior. It's just your daddy's image I have to be concerned with."

Daddy gave a snort at that.

All the while we ate beef Wellington, Enid kept saying Chicago didn't like her, because Chicago hadn't given her a chance. She said that if Chicago had gotten to know her, she would have found out they had a lot in common. "Like what?" Daddy said, laughing.

Enid didn't like it that he laughed. She said, "I was a tomboy, too, when I was Chicago's age. I could beat up any fella on my block."

I noticed that whenever she talked about being young in Brooklyn, her tone of voice became less phony and she didn't try so hard to use big words.

"Lamby," Daddy said, "Chicago is only two years younger than you are. She's not Suzy's age, and I don't think she's interested in beating up any fellas. *Is* she, Suzy?" He laughed. It was the kind of question which didn't require an answer, and he didn't seem to expect one. He was working away at his meat with his knife and fork, not looking across at me to see what I'd say.

But I said something, anyway. I said, "Chicago is getting interested in boys in a different way than beating them up."

"Fabulous!" Enid said. "She was never interested in that Scott McKay. She was just in awe of his brain."

"Did you meet him?" I asked.

"He met us," she giggled. "He barged in on us one afternoon in your father's study. Oh, was my face the color of a Tequila Sunrise! Remember, Barrybones?"

Daddy said, "Why bring that up?" in a disgusted voice.

"It just came up. I didn't *bring* it up." She nudged me with her elbow. "That's another reason Chicago and I didn't hit it off. She had to hear about Barrybones and me for the first time from that little boy friend of hers who didn't believe in knocking on closed doors."

"That's ancient history," my father said. "Drop it."

"Well, I'm glad if she's interested in boys now because I think one of her biggest problems was her Oedipus thing where your father was concerned. I mean, she didn't want anyone else to have Barrybones." She pronounced Oedipus "Oh-ead-a-puss."

My father said, "The word is pronounced 'Ed-ah-pus,' and it's a problem particular to young men and their mothers, not to young women and their fathers. That's an Electra thing."

"I could really help Chicago, if she'd only let me give her tips on how to use make-up, what kind of clothes to buy, if she's interested in boys."

"Evelyn will be more than adequate in that role," said my father.

"I didn't think she liked Evelyn," Enid said.

"They get along," I said. I looked at my father to see if he'd be pleased to hear that, but he wasn't watching me. He was watching Enid cutting her meat. She had already cut five pieces. My father can't stand it if anyone cuts more than three pieces at one time. He used to fine Chicago and me fifty cents for every piece past the third (as well as fifty cents if we ducked for our soup).

Enid felt his eyes fixed on her and she looked up at him. "What's bugging you?" she said.

"Are you cutting that meat up for some young child who doesn't know how to cut his own meat yet? Is that why you're cutting it *all* up at one time?"

"I always cut it all up at one time. Thanks for paying so much attention to my ways these past six months!"

"I should have paid more attention," said my father.

It was like watching two prizefighters spar. The only thing wrong with the picture was one of them was a lot smaller than the other.

98

I finally snapped, "Oh, *Daddy!*"

He looked very surprised. "What?" he said.

"Nothing."

"Well, *what*, Suzy?"

Was it possible that he honestly didn't know how he picked on her?

That question was never answered during my stay with them. We went to the St. Regis Room to hear some singer, after dinner, and on Sunday we just sat around in the garden and let Mrs. Bowen fix us good things to eat. Daddy didn't have much to say. He never did on Sundays until he finished *The New York Times* in its entirety. Enid talked to Fancy a lot, and I listened to more tapes.

My father called the garage for his Mercedes, and drove me to the train station.

"I'm sorry we didn't have a more exciting time planned," he said. "I guess we've just been caught up in our own sails, getting married and everything. We couldn't see much beyond our wedding day."

"It was fine," I said. "Did you call Mother about the marriage?"

"Yes. I guess she'll tell Chicago."

"Is there anything you want *me* to tell her?"

"Tell her I think she's being very stubborn," he said.

"Maybe so," I said.

"What did you say?"

"I said maybe she is being stubborn."

"Maybe?" My father gave me one of the familiar snorts he'd become famous for over the weekend.

The thing that got me was that he never really asked me anything about Chicago. He never asked What is she doing? or How is she taking to Seaville? or Does she miss me? or Is she miserable? He never picked up on my remark about her getting along better with Mother or my remark about her interest in boys. He seemed only concerned with how she felt about him, as though apart from that she had no existence which was of any importance.

I had finally found out the other part of why Daddy hated Scott McKay, too (aside from the fact he was an anarchist), and what Chicago had meant when she said Scott was the first to clue her in on Daddy. I knew how it must have hurt Chicago when she found out about Enid, because before Enid there had never been anyone in Daddy's life, really, but Chicago. I knew how much it must have hurt her to find out about it the way she had. That was Daddy's fault.

Chicago had never left Daddy; he'd done the leaving, and he hadn't bothered to make it easy for Chicago, either.

On my way back to Seaville, riding the dirty old Long Island Rail Road, I felt all turned around by the time I'd spent with Daddy. For one thing I didn't ask myself why concerning his marriage to Enid, at least I didn't ask myself why he had to marry *her*. I just kept thinking of how she called her little dog Fancy, and how she tried to have something smart to say to me about books, and I ached for her. I didn't think he was going to be very nice to her, and that was the other thing about my visit. I'd never questioned his behavior in my whole life. I'd only thought about my failings, the things I didn't measure up to, the ways I'd never be like Chicago.

Now I just wondered about him, not as Daddy, and not as the man in *Who's Who, Business Week, Fortune,* or on *Interview.* But Barry Slade, the individual.

Did I even like him anymore?

When the train pulled into Seaville, I could see Macaulay standing beside the Lincoln. It was 10:10 P.M.

"Where's Mother?" I asked him as he took my knapsack from my hands.

"She's entertaining," he said.

"On a Sunday night?"

"Yes, ma'am."

I sat up front with him and we started down toward the turn to Main Street.

"She never entertains on Sunday night," I said.

"She's entertaining this Sunday night, ma'am."

"Who?"

"A schoolmate of Miss Chicago's," he said.

"What schoolmate of Miss Chicago's?"

Macaulay said, "A colored schoolmate of Miss Chicago's. Coe is his name."

I let out a long, sinking whistle.

Macaulay pokerfaced it.

Twelve

Mrs. Leary, our housekeeper, told me that my mother and sister "and visitor" were all out in the solarium.

As I walked in that direction, I could hear Ella Fitzgerald's voice singing "Lady Be Good." Mother always tried to fit the proper mood music to the occasion. She had probably gone through her album collection to find a black singer for Roger's benefit.

Mother was also wearing one of her dresses from her "solarium wardrobe." I called it that because they were all yellow and white, and because she only wore something from that collection when she sat on the yellow-and-white wicker settee, where she was sitting as I walked in. Roger and Chicago were both in old jeans, sitting in white wicker chairs with their backs to the ocean, facing her.

Roger got up and bowed. "Suzy, hi."

"Hi, Roger. Everyone."

My mother said, "We're just enjoying some music and having a few nightcaps. Do you want a Coke?"

"No, thanks," I said. Mother was wearing hose and heels and her Gucci bracelets, doing a whole I-am-Chicago's-very-proper-mother number for Roger.

But her hand was around a glass, and not far away was the bottle of I.W. Harper and the ice bucket. That was Mother's courage.

I sat down next to Mother.

She said, "Isn't it interesting that your father actually married her? Tell us your impression of her."

"She's very nice," I said.

"With a little more effort we might get *some* idea of what she's like," said Mother.

"She's young and she's got this little dog called Fancy."

"He could have done a lot worse," Chicago said.

"I wonder," Mother said, "if there's such a thing as an adjective tutor. It might be worth the investment so one could reap the benefit of your observations in ordinary conversation."

Roger chuckled and crossed his long legs and shifted his strong, long body in the chair. He was sitting so that his arm was touching Chicago's arm, and he'd look down at her every few minutes as though there was something special about the top of her head. Her hair was growing, anyway. Otherwise the only change in Chicago seemed to be a change about Enid Rider Slade . . . a vague acceptance.

Just as I was pondering this, Chicago announced, "I called Daddy and congratulated him."

"She actually did," said Mother.

"I'm glad Daddy married someone like her."

"Why?" I said. "You used to hate her."

"I never hated her. I was just jealous of her because I'd exaggerated Daddy's importance in my life."

"Now you're going too far in the opposite direction," said my mother.

Chicago pretended not to hear that remark. She said, "I think Enid will actually be good for Daddy, because she's from the people."

"Oh, I see," said Mother, "and where was I from?"

"You're not from the people. You never worked in your life."

"I beg your pardon, Little Miss Know-it-all. I worked very hard one summer on *Vogue* magazine, as an editorial assistant. At very low pay."

"Mother, you don't have the slightest idea what I'm talking about!"

"I very definitely do have an idea and I don't fancy it one bit." Mother chunked a couple of ice cubes into her glass and poured bourbon over them.

"Daddy's doing a good thing," Chicago said. "He's finally turning his back on pig society and doing what he feels like doing."

"Yes, we very definitely need an adjective tutor," said Mother. " 'Pig society' is one of the least original expressions I've heard all day."

Then my mother addressed herself to Roger. "Tell me something," she said, "as valedictorian of your class, could you offer a prediction concerning the future of the English language?"

Roger gave another chuckle, uncrossed his legs, and leaned forward with his drink resting on his knee. He smiled at my mother. "I'm not interested in language, either. It's just subterfuge."

"Oh? Subterfuge for what?"

"For the truth about what's happening to the people."

"And what is happening to the people?"

"The pigs are keeping it all for themselves," Chicago said.

"I didn't ask *you*," said my mother. "I asked Roger."

"Well, that's pretty much my answer, too," Roger said.

"Don't let her think for you, Roger," my mother said.

"We think alike," said Roger.

"Something tells me she was there first," said my mother.

"Does it matter, Mrs. Slade?"

Ella Fitzgerald stopped singing and Johnny Mathis started crooning "Chances Are."

"My, we got all these darkies performing for us to-night," said Chicago.

Roger grinned down at her.

My mother said, "I've *always* liked Johnny Mathis."

"Me too," I said, beginning to feel a little sorry for Mother. Then I said, "Congratulations, Roger. I didn't know you were the valedictorian."

"I didn't know until yesterday," he said.

"He's refusing the distinction," said Chicago with a snide smile.

"You're *what*?" said my mother.

"I'm not going to accept, Mrs. Slade."

"Why not? I should think your family would be so very proud of you."

"They would," said Roger, "but *I* wouldn't be very proud of me. I think the grading system is unfair. Not everyone's had the same opportunity. Some of the kids go right to work after school and they're too tired at night when it comes to studying, and some others go to sleep hungry and aren't too sharp the next morning."

"But *you* made it, Roger. You'd be an example, and an inspiration."

"I'd be a lie, ma'am. I never went to the potato fields to work, or to bed hungry. My family's well-off compared to most blacks out here."

"Roger, some of our most famous men overcame obstacles."

"Mother," Chicago said, "we wouldn't expect you to understand. Roger is doing what he must for his own sake."

"It's my guess it's for your sake, at your instigation, and wholly with your motivation."

"Mrs. Slade," said Roger, "it doesn't matter who got an idea first if it's a worthwhile idea. Now, I believe Chicago's opened my eyes to some worthwhile ideas, and ma'am, it doesn't matter they were hers first."

For a while mother and Roger talked, politely, even earnestly. I sat back and watched and listened, but mostly I watched. I don't know if Mother could see but they never stopped touching. If Roger leaned forward so that his arm moved away from Chicago's arm, his leg pressed against hers. At times he put his arm across the back of her chair, and only one finger touched her back, but I could feel her feel it. The thing was, I suddenly knew what Miss Spring had meant when she'd said it was sweet and tender between Roger and Nan Richmond, but it was not really exalting to watch. There was something exalting about Roger and Chicago together. Call it chemistry, electricity, the right vibes: there was something so special about them together. Yet they were just sitting side by side.

Somewhere in the middle of "Misty," my mother suddenly stood up.

"Well, everyone, I'm going upstairs now." She put out her hand to Roger and he shook it. "I'm glad Chicago asked you here this evening, Roger Coe."

"Thank you, Mrs. Slade."

"Now I know you."

"Yes," said Roger.

"Suzy, don't stay up too late. Chicago, remember you have school, too." My mother left the solarium.

Roger sat down and put his arm around Chicago. He laughed.

"Does she always leave a room so suddenly?"

"She's just admitted she doesn't know how to handle the situation," said Chicago.

I said, "How did this all come about?"

"Macaulay ratfinked on me Saturday night. He followed me and then he came back and told Mother I was with a quote/unquote colored boy. So Mother got curious about this quote/unquote." She grinned up at Roger and I just sat there for several long seconds while they drank each other in with their eyes.

I finally said, "Did Roger come to dinner?"

"Prime ribs, Miss Nibs," Roger laughed.

"Well, how is Mother taking it?" I said.

"You just saw her. How would you say she was taking it?" said Chicago.

I said, "I don't know, but I won't forget this weekend for a long time."

They were laughing together and touching, and I felt left out. Not that I wanted them to include me. But I wanted to be included somewhere.

I did the same thing my mother did—went up to my room. I couldn't hear her television going, and I wondered if she was reading or what. But I didn't knock on her door and ask. That wasn't the kind of thing I ever did, or that she ever encouraged me to do.

Later on, from my window, I could see Roger and Chicago heading out toward the dunes with a flashlight, going for a walk. It was a bright night with a new moon, and I walked to the window to see if I could hear their laughter again before I went to sleep.

I just heard the ocean and smelled it, and standing there I saw Mother's light go out. Then I heard the music from her radio, on the table near the window. She was probably sitting in her rocker, looking out at the ocean, just as I was.

Thirteen

That Monday morning we were supposed to bring love poetry into English class. Everyone was to read a favorite.

About four kids read before Martha Crammer recited one she'd memorized. It was by Heinrich Heine, two verses from something called "Healing the Wound."

> With kisses my lips were wounded by you,
> So kiss them well again;
> And if by evening you are not through,
> You need not hurry then.
> For you have still the whole, long night,
> Darling, to comfort me.
> And what long kisses and what delight
> In such a night may be!

I still can't figure out why Martha chose that poem. It sounded as though she had some heavy affair under way with someone, when the truth was she didn't even have a date for the senior prom. Neither did I. Neither did a lot of us freshmen.

I think Mrs. Smith was slightly shocked. She's thirty, and a little old-fashioned.

"What is that supposed to mean?" she asked Martha.

"I wasn't aware it was supposed to mean anything, other than what it says," Martha said, her face becoming tomato-red.

"That poem doesn't celebrate *love*, exactly," said Mrs. Smith, sniffing as though someone had set fire to garbage somewhere in the vicinity.

"Then what does it celebrate?" Martha Crammer was as stubborn about things as her house on Main Street was big.

The next voice was a surprise. It was Lena Klein's squeaky tone piping up in this high, nervous sound. She said, "Physicality."

"What?" Martha turned to look at her.

"It celebrates the same thing a poem like 'Wild Nights' celebrates," said Lena.

"I've never even heard of 'Wild Nights'!" said Martha.

Mrs. Smith said she had never heard of "Wild Nights," either. I suppose Lena had heard Nan and me discuss it.

Lena said it was a poem by Emily Dickinson, and there was an illustrated rendering of it in the Phineas Ulin Collection, done by Fabrizio.

"We are not discussing Fabrizio!" Mrs. Smith said testily.

Martha Crammer said, "There wasn't anything dirty about the poem I read."

"There isn't anything dirty about a Fabrizio, either," Lena persisted.

Mrs. Smith said she doubted that Lena was in any

position to make such a value judgment, and Martha Crammer said only someone like Lena would read filthy things into the poem she'd read. Then both Lena and Martha began screaming at each other, and Mrs. Smith broke it up, using physical force against Lena, who was trying to pull Martha's hair.

After English everyone was talking about it, but I couldn't stay interested. All I could think about was the fact Nan hadn't shown up yet. I went to the pay phone next to the gym three times. Finally toward the end of the afternoon, I went to the principal's office. I told him I thought someone should go to Inscape and see if everything was all right.

He told me Nan's mother had called. Nan wasn't well. They were probably at the doctor's.

Something else bothered me, too. I hadn't seen Roger or Chicago all day at school. The last glimpse I'd had of Chicago was early that morning. Her head had emerged from the covers long enough to shut off the alarm, then she'd fallen back asleep.

I'd managed to ask her, "What time did you get back from your walk last night?"

She'd managed to answer, "What year do you think your voice will give out finally, from questioning people day and night around the clock?"

After school, as I was heading for the library, this old dark-blue Buick with white paint smeared across one fender pulled over and stopped. There was a squirrel's tail hanging from the antenna of the radio, and the radio was playing loud. I saw about six black faces looking at me, and I don't know which one said, "Have you seen Roger?" but I do know it was a female voice.

"No," I said, stupidly adding, "Roger Coe?"

"Yes, Roger Coe, Starch Face. You know the name?"

"Of course I know the name."

"Of course you know the name," the voice came back imitating my whine.

I started walking a little faster, but the car was gliding along right beside me.

"You tell Roger Coe some of his friends were looking for him, do you hear?"

"Yes," I said.

"Tell Roger Coe some of his *black* friends were looking for him," whoever she was said. "Hear? You tell Roger Coe that for us."

"I hear," I said.

Then I got the nerve to stop and turn around and look at them. I said, "Do you all know where Nan Richmond is?"

"Oh yawl. Do yawl know where Nanny is, yawl?" A few of them laughed uproariously.

"I meant all of you, or any of you," I said. "Do you know where she is?"

"Come on out to Inscape and find out for yourself, Whitey," said a boy's voice.

I said, "I might just do that, thank you," but I doubted that I sounded very convincing or confident.

"Oh, I love your manners," the girl's voice again. The laughter again.

Then the car started up fast and raced forward. I could see a trail of dust and hear the wheels squeal on the turn.

When I got to the library, there was a strange undercurrent running through the place. Mrs. Timberlake was rushing around on tiptoe conferring with the other librarians, and a disheveled-looking man with bright-blue bloodshot eyes was standing by Check Out passing his straw hat back and forth from one hand to the other. He was bald and potbellied, and his suit needed to be pressed. It was a brown-and-white pinstripe suit that had seen better days, but he looked all the shabbier because he was wearing old white sneakers, and an all-white tie that wasn't all white any longer.

Mrs. Timberlake spotted me and rushed across to whisper, "Have you heard from Nan?"

"She's sick," I said. "She won't be here today."

"Have you heard from her?"

"She's sick," I said again. "She wasn't in school."

Mrs. Timberlake bared her teeth and spoke very slowly and with quite a lot of hostility. "Have you *heard* from her, Suzy? Answer me."

"I haven't heard from her, no."

"That was what I asked you in the first place!" She was actually snarling at me.

"What's the matter?" I said. "What's going on around here?"

"Of all the days for him to show up!" said Mrs. Timberlake.

"Who?"

"Him." Mrs. Timberlake nodded her head in the direction of the disheveled-looking man. "Lester Quinn."

"Lester Quinn?" I stared across at him.

"We're handling an emergency, and *he* turns up like a bad penny."

For a few seconds I couldn't look away from him. I couldn't find the baby-faced, innocent-eyed, laughing lieutenant in his face anywhere.

Then I heard Miss Spring's soft voice say to Mrs. Timberlake, "I can't stay this afternoon. *You* understand."

"I'm afraid you'll have to stay for a while."

"You could telephone me if anything of importance comes up."

"Something of importance has come up! As you very well know! I'm going to call a staff meeting."

"Oh no." Miss Spring seemed on the verge of tears.

"Everyone will have to attend. Particularly you, Gwen! I'm very sorry!"

"All right, Mrs. Timberlake," Miss Spring said. "If you say so," she sighed and then she noticed me standing there. She touched my elbow with her fingers. "Do you see who's over there, Suzy?"

"Yes. Did he just arrive?"

"Oh honey, the years haven't been gentle with him, have they?"

114

She was watching him from across the room through her thick Coke-bottle-bottom glasses, a small, wistful smile playing at her lips. She had on very dark lipstick and pancake make-up, a fresh white dickey with a long hand-knit navy-blue sweater over it, a long strand of pearls knotted once, and a pleated, plaid skirt. Saddle shoes, socks. She smelled of Tweed, and her nails had been newly manicured and painted very red.

I said, "Did he just get here?"

"Just now. Oh, poor Papa-doodle, what has he seen and been through that I couldn't help him with, that I didn't even know about?"

Mrs. Timberlake appeared again long enough to say, "Children's Room in five minutes, Gwen."

"Come and meet him, Suzy," said Miss Spring. "Oh honey, be tender to him. He's seen such a lot; it's written all over his face. His eyes break my heart."

We walked across to him and Miss Spring took my hand, did a sort of swinging step as though she were presenting me at court, and said, "Lester Quinn, I would like you to meet Suzy Slade."

"How do you do, sweetie," he said.

I said, "I've heard a lot about you."

"About *me*?" He gave a little deprecating chuckle and rubbed his nose with the back of his hand.

"Of course about you, Papa-doodle," said Miss Spring. "You were always in our thoughts."

He said something which sounded like, "Oh hell,

Gwen, honey," and then he said, "Well, that's very nice and thoughtful of you, I must say."

I excused myself and went back to the staff room. Two of the senior assistants were buzzing with Mrs. Timberlake, and again I felt a mysterious undercurrent.

Then everyone but a junior assistant and me filed into the Children's Room and shut the door.

I walked down to the fiction cart and started putting away books. Then I heard someone put change into the pay telephone, quite a lot of change: there was a clanging for several seconds.

Next: Lester Quinn's voice.

He said, "Hello? Grace? It's me. Yes. I'm in Seaville."

I moved closer to the phone without being seen, hidden in the stacks.

"I haven't asked her yet," he said, "but she's in a very friendly mood."

Then he listened for a while and I stayed very still.

Next: "I might not get the full amount, but she's good for some of it, I'm pretty sure."

He listened some more and then he said in such an earnest voice, "Oh honey, honey, don't worry about anything, honey, my sweet."

I didn't hear the good-by, if there was one. I didn't want to listen to any more of the conversation.

Fourteen

My mother likes to say that bravery isn't tested during big moments but in little, everyday ones, in the way one faces people and faces up to problems with them. I have always been a bit of a coward, preferring to avoid scenes, and hating to see anyone I know get hurt.

I guess it was this cowardice that kept me from any confrontation with Miss Spring after she came out of the staff meeting. I hid back in the foreign language stacks where almost no one goes, and waited until she left with Lester Quinn.

I was afraid she'd say, "Well, Mama-doodle, what did you think of him?"

I was afraid she'd tell me he was back to stay, just like she'd always known he would be.

I didn't even see her face, but I did see some of the other staff members' faces. They were all very grim.

I had no idea what crisis was taking place at the library by the time I finished work for the day. I only knew there was something important underfoot, something heavy.

It was a beautiful June afternoon; the sun was out, and I told myself that was the reason I was going for a long bicycle ride. But I knew better. I was restless and expectant, without any reason I could think of: just a feeling. Maybe there's such a thing as "full-moon days." My mother claims that on the night of a full moon she gets tense and sad. I didn't feel sad, exactly, but I felt worried. What seemed most on my mind was getting to Nan, seeing her, in person, having some reassurance she was okay. I wasn't sure whether it was because of what was going on with Chicago and Roger that I wanted to see her, or because Mrs. Timberlake had kept stressing the verb *hear* when she asked about Nan. Had I *heard* from her?

I rode my bike out to Inscape, by the bay, looking for 29 Peter's Lane. It was a large, white, wooden house, two-story, with a long front porch.

As I walked up the path a thin black woman came to the screen door and I said, "Mrs. Richmond?"

"Yes?"

"I'm Suzy Slade. I work with Nan at the library."

Mrs. Richmond came out on the porch and looked at my face in a careful way, unsmiling. She said, "Nan doesn't work at the library anymore."

"No one there knows that," I said. "Did she tell anyone at the library?"

"She wrote them a letter."

"Is she all right?" I said.

"I don't know. Is she? I just don't know what's got into her."

"Is she sick?"

"Physically ill? No. She's all right."

"At school they said she was sick."

"They'll be getting a letter, too. Nan quit school."

"*Quit* school? Before final exams?"

"She quit. She says forever. She took a job today at Tout Va Bien. A waitress job." All of a sudden Mrs. Richmond bent her head and began to cry softly.

I said, "Oh, no. No." Somehow I was very aware of the fact I hadn't asked what happened, why, what was going on; perhaps I feared the answer.

But in her next breath Mrs. Richmond let me know she didn't know the answer. "I can't get her to talk with me," she said. "She always confided in me, but not now. Do you know what it could be?"

I said, "I guess I do," and sighed, half with desperation and half with relief that I realized I was going to level with Mrs. Richmond, to face up to something for once in my life. "Roger has been seeing my sister," I said. "They've been seeing each other for a couple of weeks now."

"I see."

"Nan probably just found out about it."

"I see."

"My own mother just found out about it."

"And you?"

"I found out about it about a week ago."

There was a silence and then I said, "I swore to my sister I wouldn't say anything about it, not to anyone."

"I understand," said Mrs. Richmond. "I understand that

kind of a promise." She sighed and stared out at the bay with tired brown eyes. "I just don't understand why Nanny'd quit school, take a job as a waitress. Roger's leaving is a blow, yes. A blow. But to quit school so suddenly, take a job waiting on people, just like that." She snapped her fingers and for a while the only other sound in the silence that followed was a clothesline bird cackling overhead in the white pine tree.

"I'm sorry," I said.

"Nan's at work out there now. I've never been out there."

"I was out there once with my mother for dinner."

"Is it a nice place?"

"It's right on the ocean and it has violins and fancy food."

"I can't see her doing that, can you? Waiting on tables?"

"She had a perfectly good job," I said.

"She said it wasn't a money-making job."

"Well, she was right about that."

"A money-making job," said Mrs. Richmond. "Nan talking like that."

"Tell her I came by to see her, would you?" I said.

"Thank you for coming by, Suzy."

"I'm sorry," I said again.

When I finally got home, Mrs. Leary told me my mother was in the saffron garden and would like to see me.

The saffron garden is filled only with yellow flowers; yellow is my mother's favorite color. There is everything in that garden from tiny buttercups to giant sunflowers, soft yellow roses and bitter-smelling marigolds. My mother doesn't go there a lot, but when she's in the mood to garden, she does.

She didn't say Hello or How are you or How was school today or anything. She said, "Suzy, how well do you know Nan Richmond?"

I shrugged. That was my main gesture that spring. It was Shrug Spring. "I know her well enough."

"Do you trust her?"

"With what?"

"Do you trust her, not necessarily with something, but do you trust her?"

"Yes, I trust her."

"There's been a theft from the library of a very valuable property."

"That's what all the mystery is about."

"I'm not going into all the details but I'd like reassurance from you that you know nothing whatsoever about it."

"I don't and Nan doesn't either."

"Just speak for yourself."

"You asked me about Nan."

"I know I asked you about Nan, but now just answer for yourself."

"I have. What book is it?"

"It doesn't matter, so long as you know nothing about it."

"That isn't why Nan quit the library."

"I never said it was."

"It isn't why she quit school, either. I could tell you why she did both things."

"I'm not really all that interested in Nan Richmond's personal life," said my mother. Then she said, "Go make yourself pretty for dinner, Suzy. Chicago won't be dining with us, but Adele Crammer is coming by to discuss politics with me."

"To discuss politics with you?"

"You heard me."

"Where's Chicago going to be?"

"She's taking a lunch to the beach."

I didn't say anything. I might have sighed. Tiredly.

My mother said, "That'll run its own course."

"In the meantime, some people are being hurt," I said.

"Whom do you mean?"

"Before all this happened, Roger's girl friend was Nan Richmond. Did you know that?"

"No, I didn't know that."

"Well, she was."

"I see."

"Nan's quit school. She's quit school and she's quit her job at the library."

"Why?"

"*Why?* What kind of a question is that? I'm telling you why."

"I knew she'd quit the library. Mrs. Timberlake told me that when she phoned about the theft."

"She doesn't think Nan took it, does she?"

"She has no idea *who* took it."

"Well, it's the last thing Nan would do. She's upset about losing Roger. She's just giving up because of Roger's running off with Chicago."

My mother glanced across at me coolly, holding a cutting of a yellow rose called Apogee.

"Suzy," she said as though her patience was greatly strained, "men have died and worms have eaten them, as the old saying goes, but not for love. I'm afraid that goes for women, too."

"What do you mean!" I began to holler. "What are you saying?"

"Calm down! I'm simply telling you that anyone who quits school because she lost her boy friend didn't *want* to go to school. To use your own ill-structured vocabulary, it's a cop-out."

"Nobody wanted to go to school more than Nan!" I said angrily.

"Then she'd be going to school, my dear."

"God, I hate white people sometimes! We are nothing but a bunch of Starch Faces! Smug, awful, self-centered, idiotic, boring, Starch Faces!"

My mother said quietly, "I agree. At times you can say the same for blacks, yellows, greens, reds, et cetera."

"Why can't you see what Chicago's doing?"

"Chicago can't see what Chicago's doing either," said

my mother, "so she's not really guilty of the injustices you claim for her."

"Right!" I snapped. "Innocent Little Chicago!"

My mother looked me firmly in the eye. "Suzy, let this thing run its course. This is not your business, and you may as well get that straight immediately."

"Can't I have an opinion?"

"You've had altogether too many. Give your mind a rest, dear."

"Sometimes I feel like just saying the hell with life," I muttered.

"Acids stain you, nooses give, you might as well live, as Dorothy Parker wrote once. Make yourself pretty for dinner, Suzy."

I groaned.

Chicago's knapsack was on her bed when I walked into our bedroom. It was packed to the top.

The shower was running. I walked into the steamy bathroom and said, "You look like you're packing for a weekend, not a picnic."

"Hey, don't you love all the excitement over a missing painting?"

"Is it a painting?"

"It's a Fabrizio."

"You're kidding."

"Uh uh. It was swiped from that precious collection where only the elite may trespass."

Then Chicago said, "I also love Adele Crammer coming here tonight to persuade Mother to help her run for town supervisor! Adele Crammer!"

I was trying to digest the news that the theft was a Fabrizio from the Phineas Ulin Collection.

That explained all the hubbub at the library, and Miss Spring's involvement.

"Don't you adore the idea of Adele Crammer running for office?"

"It doesn't bother me," I managed to answer.

"Nothing bothers you if you can stand to have dinner with Adele Crammer. My God, Suzy, she's horrible, running around in her mink coats in the daytime, wearing all the jewelry that's ever been given her all at one time. She's grotesque."

"She's Martha's mother," I said, making little sense, feeling stupid. "I don't really have a choice."

"Everyone has a choice," said Chicago.

I decided not to continue the conversation. I was on the verge of mentioning something about her own choice, and how much it had cost Nan. I walked out of the bathroom and went across the hall to sit on my bed, wondering if I wanted to try and puzzle over things, or if I wanted to just take a long hot shower, as Chicago was doing, and put everything out of my head.

My eyes returned to the bulging knapsack.

On sheer impulse I thrust my hand inside, feeling around, curious at what all Chicago was taking to the beach for her picnic with Roger. I felt a pair of jeans, a shirt, shoes, a sweater, and then my fingers touched something they'd touched before.

I pulled the knapsack wider apart and peered down at Fabrizio's small painting of "Wild Nights."

Fifteen

"Small children ask to be excused from dinner immediately after they have finished dessert," my mother is fond of pointing out. "When you're ready to linger on for a little while, you're ready to grow up."

I was pretending I was ready to grow up, sitting in a white wicker armchair in the solarium, while Mrs. Leary served coffee to Mother and Mrs. Crammer, and Ovaltine to me.

During the soup course at dinner, I had heard the sounds of Chicago's and Roger's motorcycles tearing away. Mother had commented, "I guess Chicago is picnicking farther down the beach," and stayed her great cool self, no indication she was at all ruffled by that idea, no hint Chicago was with anyone in particular but some friend.

I hadn't been able to bring myself to confront Chicago with what I'd found in her knapsack. I could not believe that she and Roger thought stealing from the P-U collection was a fun prank or a daring adventure—I didn't know what they thought. I only knew I had to do something, somehow. I was trying to figure out just what that would be: what and how, and all by myself?

Mother and Mrs. Crammer had a few martinis before dinner, some wine with dinner, and now Mother was serving them a drink called a Rusty Nail. Mrs. Crammer was a plump, gray-haired woman with good legs, which were spread out gracefully across the wicker chaise. She was becoming a little flushed from having a good time, fondling her pearls as she talked, and giggling with my mother. She didn't look at all like Martha, but more like the little pug she'd brought with her, snub-nosed and round-eyed and slightly petulant.

Despite the fact I was there with my Ovaltine, trying to indicate that I was ready to linger on and grow up, they were ignoring me, although my name came up in conversation occasionally.

For example: on the subject of Enid.

"It's a pity, really," Evelyn Slade talking. "Suzy says she's this redheaded creature with orange toenails, who thought *Vogue* was a weekly, and she has a dog called Fancy."

I said, "I didn't say just that. I said nice things about her, too." I felt like a traitor to Enid. Out of everything I'd told Mother about her, she'd taken a few facts and twisted them into the one ugly picture.

127

"A dog called Fancy!" Martha Crammer's mother exclaimed. "Oh, how pathetic!" (Her own dog was named Caviar.)

"Barry's in some state of mild psychosis, in my opinion," said my mother. "I think he's in the midst of a form of very serious nervous breakdown."

"It *could* indeed be a form of very serious nervous breakdown."

"Of course it could. Oh, could and *is*, Adele. Let's face it. Why on earth would someone like Barry even look at such a creature!"

"Isn't love odd, Evelyn?" Mrs. Crammer remarked, smoothing her flower-print dress across her knees with pudgy diamond-bedecked hands. "It doesn't give a damn what anyone else thinks. It just does as it damn pleases!"

My mother got up and went to slip on a tape of boring cornet solos. She was angry. I could tell by the tape selection, and her walk. She hated the fact Mrs. Crammer had veered away from the idea Daddy was psychotic, and summed it up as love.

Mother turned up the cornet music very loud and Mrs. Crammer glanced across at me, I suppose to see the expression on my face, and judge whether or not this was an everyday occurrence.

I said, "Mother? I have to go see Miss Spring. Can Macaulay take me there?"

"Love it is not!" my mother answered Mrs. Crammer, swishing angrily back to her chair with a new Rusty Nail she'd made herself at the teacart. Then, to me, "Don't stay at Miss Spring's. I've had Macaulay out all day and he's probably très fatigué."

"Merci, maman," I said.

"Do you often listen to cornet music?" Mrs. Crammer was asking my mother as I left.

I told Macaulay to wait for me. Then I headed for the outside steps leading to Miss Spring's second-floor apartment. The owners of Coffee Beings were barbecuing chicken in their backyard, and they gave me a wave and a smile.

Miss Spring's front door was open. I rang the bell and peered through the screen to see if I could see her.

The phonograph was playing, a woman singing, "I came here to talk for Joe, he wants me to let you know, he can't keep that date with you tonight."

"Miss Spring?" I called. "It's me. Suzy Slade."

There was no answer, and I began to fear I had come at the wrong time. I thought of how quiet my father's house was that Saturday afternoon, after lunch, when Fancy and I were downstairs, and they were upstairs and not fighting anymore.

I said, "Miss Spring?" and almost did not wait for an answer but had started to turn when I heard her say, "Well, Mama-doodle, what brings you here at this hour?"

"Macaulay brought me," I said. "He's waiting for me."

"Do you want to come in, is that it?" She was standing

in the shadows of her kitchen. I could not see her well through the screen.

"Yes, please, it's important, or I wouldn't have interrupted you."

"You didn't interrupt anything," she said. "Lester Quinn has come and gone."

She held open the screen door for me. She was wearing a worn terry-cloth robe which had seen better days, faded blue and frayed. She looked very pale. I realized what was different about her face: it was the first time I had ever seen her without make-up. She had on a pair of mules that slapped the bottoms of her feet as she walked back across the kitchen and through the beaded room divider to her makeshift dining room. There was a glass of half-finished beer on the round oak table.

She sat down and cupped the glass with her hand, barely looking at me.

"Sometimes your own heart puts up such a high wall around you, you can't see over it to reality," she said. She took a swallow of her beer. "Do you want a glass of cranberry juice?"

"No, ma'am." I was about to say again that Macaulay was waiting, but I couldn't.

"Cranberry juice fights impurities in the urine, did you know that?"

"No, ma'am."

"So does a healthy love life."

"Ma'am?"

"I said so does a healthy love life, which doesn't describe my life these past Rip van Winkle years, Oh, sit down. Don't stand around acting moronic."

"I'm a little nervous, that's all."

"Why should you be nervous? I should be nervous. Nervous and bereft and half-crazy with pain, but I sit here drinking a beverage I all but detest, because I'm going to drink all night, and I can't last all night on gin or rum, or vodka, or Scotch."

I said, "I'm sorry, Miss Spring."

"I know you are. It was good of you to come."

"I didn't exactly come because I was sorry, ma'am."

"I know you didn't come because you were sorry. You came because you're a good friend. You came to stand by me. You came to see me through it. It doesn't matter. You came and you're here."

"Yes, ma'am," I said, feeling more and more rotten by the moment.

"Did you see him somewhere in town, is that it? Is he in town tying on a rip-snorter, is that it?"

I said, "I don't know, ma'am."

"Did you just know to come?"

I shrugged. An all-time record for Shrug Spring.

"He wanted to borrow money from me," she said.

"Yes, ma'am."

"That's all he wanted, Mama-doodle. His precious wife is ill, and he has no one to turn to, since his credit rating at the bank is at an infamous nadir."

"Did you lend him any?"

"Yes, of course."

"Oh, Miss Spring, why?"

"Do you think his wanting a loan could puncture a delusion that has been in existence since the end of World War II?"

"Do you still love him?"

"I love him more because love made him humble and humiliate himself and embarrass me and hurt me, and I understand that kind of love. It's the only kind I do understand."

"Yes, ma'am. I know."

"It's too bad such a compelling love wasn't directed my way. But that would have made things even and fair and not at all like life. Oh, Suzy."

"What, ma'am?"

She said a word I'd never heard her say before, one of Chicago's four-letter words.

Then she said, "We've still got to hang in there, Mamadoodle, haven't we? No matter, no matter: just hang in there."

I had to tell her why I had come. I blurted it out quite suddenly, rat-a-tat-tat, machine-gun style. "My sister and Roger took the Fabrizio. I saw it in my sister's knapsack."

She didn't seem to be listening. She was looking at her beer and shaking her head. She had removed her thick glasses and was rubbing her eyes.

"Did you hear what I said, Miss Spring?"

Still she didn't answer me.

I said, "They're at a picnic on the beach. Macaulay could help us find them and we could talk to them."

132

Without much emotion, in a quiet, tired tone, she said, "Call the police. You know where the phone is."

"Ma'am?"

"I said call the police station. They have a record of the theft from the Phineas Ulin Collection."

"Miss Spring," I said, "do you want to hear what I think happened?"

"No," she said softly.

"You don't?"

"I don't care what you think happened. Obviously what you think happened has something to do with the latest disappearance of this painting, and I'm not in investigative work. I'm a librarian, Mama-doodle, no more, no less."

I said, "But I think Nan's involved in this, too."

"I wouldn't be surprised, Mama-doodle."

"But I don't think she knew what she was doing. I think it's more complicated than it looks."

She took another swallow of beer without looking at me.

"Nan's running from something," I said.

There was a long silence.

Then Miss Spring said, "Do you want me to do it? Or will you do it?"

"Do what, ma'am?"

"Call the police," she said.

"Can't we figure out something to do besides call the police?"

"I'm through figuring out things to do, Mama-doodle."

"I can see why, I guess."

"No, you can't. You can't see anything. You're no

better than Lester Quinn is. You have your immediacies, and he has his. I am not supposed to have any. I am supposed to aid and assist people who have them, but I am not supposed to have any myself."

I said, "Can't we go and look for them and ask them to give it back?"

"It is stolen property, Suzy, no matter the approach to it."

"I don't know if I can call the police against my own sister," I said.

Miss Spring didn't say anything.

"I hope you don't think *I* had anything to do with it," I said. "I didn't. And I didn't have anything to do with its other disappearance."

"Suzy," said Miss Spring. "I don't give a tinker's dam, honey, what is going down the road right now. All I know is that I'm a car wreck smack-dab in the middle, broken and bleeding and, more's the pity, still drawing deep breaths. How many times am I going to be run over by the rest of you out driving in your big hurries?"

I said, "I see what you mean."

"Not now you don't," she said, "but one day you'll look back on this and you will see."

I stood up. Miss Spring was playing a record featuring a trumpet. I said, "I'm going now. You can call the police, if you have to, but I can't."

"This is Bunny Berrigan playing and singing," said Miss Spring.

We both listened for a moment. "I've flown around the world in a plane. I set a revolution in Spain, and the North Pole I have charted, still I can't get started with you."

"Good-by, Miss Spring," I said.

She said, "Don't let the screen door slam behind you Mama-doodle. I hate that noise more than any other."

"I won't," I promised.

Macaulay was leaning against the fender, smoking a cigarette.

"I'm ready to go home now," I said.

"Yes, ma'am." He held the door open for me. Then he tossed away his cigarette and went around front to get in the driver's seat.

"Fasten your seat belt," I said.

"That doesn't sound much like you, Miss Suzy," he said. "I've never known you to fasten yours before."

I said, "I never thought I needed one before."

Sixteen

The next day Nan and I were both sitting in the corridor of the police station. She was wearing the green-and-white Tout Va Bien uniform. She had been called from work, as I had been from an afternoon class.

"Hello, Nan."

She only said, "It's you," in a voice I could hardly hear.

"Are you mad at me?"

She looked up at the ceiling, rolling her eyes as though to indicate the question was not even worthy of an answer. She was mad, all right. She was slumped down beside me, and she began looking at her own wrists as though they were something new to her.

I said, "Do *you* know what this is all about, what my sister and Roger wanted with that painting?"

"You're here to see the big detective man, aren't you? Well, when I tell the man, you can listen in, honey, because I don't like to do the same old tap routine twice in a row."

"Nan," I said, "I'm in trouble, too. I was the one who started the whole thing by showing you the Fabrizio in the first place."

"You watch and see who's in trouble and who isn't," she said. "You want to bet who's in trouble and who isn't?"

I said, "Miss Spring will never trust me again."

"Owl Eyes will trust you again. Don't you worry your pointed blond head over that unlikely prospect."

I said, "And I haven't got any control over Chicago, if that's what's bugging you."

"The trouble with you people is you don't have any control, period. Greed controls you. You want it all."

"I'm not that way," I said. "I don't think I'm that way."

"You're all that way," she said.

"I can see why you'd think so."

"Never mind seeing why I do anything. Mind your own business. Get back to all the thrills and high callings of Ocean Road. Leave me alone."

"Oh, Nan," I started to try and reason with her, but I didn't get a chance to finish. Detective Ludlum was beckoning for us to enter his office. I followed Nan, wondering where the jails were. They were holding Roger, since they had picked up both of them last night. Chicago had come home a short while after their arrest. Mother had sprung her on $250 bail. But Roger was being held for $1000.

Daddy was on his way in a private plane to Seaville from Washington, D.C. That was the word from Mother when I had called the house at noon.

Mother had said, "You did a very courageous thing last night, Suzy."

I told her, "It wasn't my idea to call the police. It was Miss Spring's."

"Nevertheless, you went to Miss Spring, and that took courage."

"You mean to see that my own sister was arrested?"

"Suzy, you know very well what I mean! In the long run you helped Chicago by stopping something that could have grown far more serious."

"I doubt that she'll see it that way," I said. I hadn't seen my sister since her return from the police station.

She had slept in a guest room and skipped school.

Mother said to just concentrate on the fact I did the right thing.

"I wonder how Daddy will feel about it," I said.

"I don't know that Daddy *can* feel anymore," said Mother.

The detective's office was small and messy, filled with empty coffee containers, cigarette butts, wax paper that sandwiches had been wrapped in, and piles of dirty typewritten paper.

There was a man standing by the window, picking his teeth, wearing a blue sport shirt outside his pants.

"My partner, Detective Shaw," said Ludlum.

Nan didn't say anything. I said, "Hi."

"Hi. Which one of you removed the painting from the Phineas Ulin Collection?"

Nan still didn't talk. I said, "I saw it in my sister's knapsack and told Miss Spring about it."

"What were you doing going through her knapsack?" said Detective Shaw.

It was my turn not to answer. Nan spoke up then. "She was snooping through her things, no doubt."

"Well, I'm not proud of it," I said. That was the Understatement of the Year.

The detective said to Nan, "You took it from the library then?"

"Yes."

"Why?"

"I thought I was borrowing it. I borrowed it once before for him to see, and that's all I thought I was doing again."

"When did you learn differently?"

"He was supposed to bring it back to me that night. He said he wasn't returning it at all, not until the library agreed to certain things."

"Like?"

"Like open stacks," Nan said. "No payment for library cards. A bookmobile for poor people and isolated ones. A larger black history section, and more black fiction. Lots of things."

Detective Shaw said, "And where was the library supposed to get the funds to set up this sort of operation?"

Nan shrugged. "I only know what he wanted them to do, not how they were supposed to do it."

Detective Ludlum said, "They drew up quite a list of demands. They were calling themselves T.P.S., standing for The People Speak."

"Why not T.T.P.S., The Two People Speak?" said Detective Shaw. "Or were three or four or five in on this thing?" He looked at me. "Were you in on it?"

"No, sir."

He looked at Nan. "Were you?"

"No, sir. It was just Roger and her, but it was mainly her."

"Chicago Slade?"

Nan nodded enthusiastically. "In on it, responsible for it."

"Go on," Detective Shaw urged.

"Roger wouldn't dream that up," Nan said. "That's Little Miss Muffet from Ocean Road, climbed down from her web and dressed up like a revolutionary, ready to kidnap a painting."

"What makes you so sure?" said Shaw.

"I know Roger Coe. That's all. I *know* him."

"When you knew he wasn't going to return the painting, why didn't you notify the police?"

She shot me a dirty look while she answered, "I'm not the type can turn my own in."

"You would have helped him by doing it, don't you see that?"

"I was going to work to help him pay for it, help him that way," Nan said. "If he could pay the library for it, then she could do what she wanted with it."

Detective Ludlum said, "The library wanted the painting back, not the money it was worth."

Nan said, "Money's the next best thing, though."

"How well do you know this Chicago Slade?"

"I don't know her at all well," said Nan. She gave me another dirty look. "I worked side by side with her sister, to whom I used to confide my fondest and wildest, but I was never let in on what was taking place between my man and her sister!" There was a glint of cold rage from her dark eyes, and then she turned her face from mine.

I leaned forward in my chair and tried to say directly to her, "I didn't know about it for very long."

"Any long is too long," she said, looking at me with cold eyes. I had to look away.

Detective Ludlum said, "Did Miss Suzanne Slade have anything to do with any of this, other than to find the painting in her sister's knapsack?"

"As far as I know she's innocent, and pure white." Nan said the last part mockingly.

Detective Ludlum said I could go, and offered to drive me home.

I said, "I'm going to the library. Business as usual." I felt like letting the tears I was holding back burst forth—anything to change the expression on Nan's face, to wipe away the hatred showing there.

But I doubt that my tears would have made a dent.

I walked out of there weighed down by guilt, not just at the feeling I'd let Nan down, but also because I'd gone through Chicago's things, and that had caused all this. I didn't care what I'd saved her from in the long run; in the short run I'd become a supersly turncoat snoop.

It wasn't really my idea to carry on with business as usual. I'd have just as soon skipped that afternoon at the library. But my mother had insisted, at the end of our phone conversation that noon.

"In a crisis," she had said, "you do the same as you do every day, as far as possible. That's what holds things together. Routine is fiber, and in a crisis, fiber binds."

Seventeen

When I got home that night, Chicago was sitting out in the solarium with my mother and father, and Roger's grandfather, B.C. The Coe truck was parked in our driveway. Painted on its sides were EAT WELL TO FEEL GOOD INSIDE (Coe's Barbecue Place) and CALL US TO LOOK GOOD OUTSIDE (Coe Landscaping).

Mrs. Leary took my drink order, one Coca-Cola, and I sat down across from Chicago.

"He's a good boy, Mr. Slade," B.C. was saying. "His grandmother only stays alive to see him march across that stage to get his diploma, head of his class."

Chicago said, "What a beautiful black woman she is, too."

B.C. frowned at Chicago, and his mouth twisted in a grimace before he said, "Black's not a word I use. You and Roger use words I don't need to use."

"Words like what, B.C.?" said Chicago.

"Never mind," said my father, and my mother said, "That's right, Chicago, drop it."

I looked at Mother, who was sipping a bourbon and

soda. There was something different about her. I couldn't decide what it was. She didn't look the same.

B.C. continued anyway. "Words like revolution. I don't need that word."

"We all need that word," Chicago said.

"I don't, I most surely don't, Miss Chicago."

"Don't call me Miss Chicago. I don't call you Mr. B.C."

"Chicago!" my father snapped. "Let me handle this. Hush." He softened his tone when Chicago glared across at him.

"Why are you so in love with the word 'handle'?" Chicago asked him mockingly.

"Now that *is* a word needed here," B.C. said. "I wouldn't be here if there wasn't something we had to handle. There's trouble here to handle, and there's a question of a lot of money here. Practical things here."

"We can manage Roger's bail," my mother said to B.C. "Don't worry about that." For some reason she looked more sophisticated and slightly more remote.

"I'd be most grateful, Mrs. Slade. I promise you he's worth anything you risk. I believe I can promise that. Up until now he was never mixed up in anything like this, never thought that way at all. I don't think he thinks that way now. Don't think he's *doing* his own thinking."

"We're glad to make his bail," said my father.

"I would have made it myself, but one thousand dollars is a sum of money I don't have on hand. Roger's dad don't, either."

"It's only because Roger's black he has a bail that high," Chicago said.

"Chicago," my father said, "we can do nicely without you, while we tie up these loose ends."

Chicago stood up. "Roger is doing his own thinking."

B.C. shook his head negatively. I stood up, too, eager to get away from the mounting tension.

"You girls should be very proud of your father," said B.C.

"Why?" Chicago said. "Because he's rich?"

"Because he's kind," B.C. answered. "Because he's a Christian man."

I said, "I'm glad to know you, Mr. Coe."

"Pleased to meet you, too," he said. "Thanks to you this thing was nipped in the bud, thanks to you."

"We'll strike again," said Chicago.

My father glanced up at her with sudden, flashing eyes. "That's what you think."

Chicago gave a little salute in B.C.'s direction and we took off.

On the way upstairs, Chicago nudged me in the ribs. I was afraid to turn around and see her face, afraid that the accusations would begin, and the anger at my going through her things, then turning her in.

But she was laughing. "Hey, did you notice our old lady?"

"What in particular?"

"You didn't see the black dress?"

"Was that what made her seem different?"

"All the years Dad practically begged her on bended knees to wear black, and now she puts on a black dress."

I said, "Why?"

"Oh, Suzy, you know why."

"Why?"

"She wants to prove something to herself, just like B.C. wants to prove something to himself. The whole world is trying to prove things to themselves."

"Prove what?"

"Well, Mom's trying to prove she can get Dad back."

"No."

"Of course."

"She doesn't want Daddy back."

"I know she doesn't want him back. She never wanted him to begin with. But she wants to prove to herself she can have him back if she wants him back."

"That's awfully small."

"I'm beginning to think the so-called big people in the world are all awfully small, and the so-called little people are the ones who are big."

"Chicago," I said, "you don't even know many so-called little people."

She ignored this statement of fact. "Look at B.C. tonight with his bootlicking colored folks act. He's trying to prove to himself he's still a good nigger that white folks would let past the back door, even though he probably could have made Roger's bail himself."

145

"Why wouldn't he then?"

"He doesn't trust Roger anymore. He doesn't want to risk all that hard-earned money. And he wants to impress the fact on Dad that he's a good nigger."

"I think he just loves Roger and wants to help him."

"If B.C. really gave a damn about Roger, he'd stop shuffling across our floors with his hand out," Chicago said. "Roger would hate that."

"You're too hard on people, Chicago," I said.

She said, "I'm just beginning to figure people out. It's not a pretty picture."

It was hot in our room. It was late afternoon and there wasn't much of a breeze from the ocean. We both stripped and stretched out on our beds naked, staring up at the ceiling and listening to the waves down on the beach.

It was my favorite time of day, and I began to appreciate how much I liked being there with Chicago, watching the brightness of the sun start to fade, the sky get that red-beginning-of-sunset color, and smelling the sea spray. Chicago's cynicism didn't bother me so much lately; all she was was scared and trying to fight her way past it.

She said, "One thing I've learned about life is that if you love someone, you change. You have to. Maybe I was just mouthing a lot of stuff Scott McKay taught me, until I met Roger, but then I saw the truth. I mean, just because Roger's black he's treated as an inferior, automatically, any place outside of Seaville, and some places inside of Seaville. So I changed, grew to believe things I was just giving lip service to. And Roger's changed, too. I raised

146

his social consciousness, Suzy. He was just this jock, you know?"

"This valedictorian jock," I said.

"Oh, I don't mean he was just a jock. Rog is a brain. But he had no social consciousness." She was smoothing her hand along her stomach, talking at me with her eyes closed.

I said, "Maybe you do have to change when you fall in love. Mom says Daddy's been a missing person since he met Enid."

"That's a good way to put it," Chicago said. "You lose your old self, you shed it. Old friends who knew you well can't find you anymore."

"I wonder if I'll ever fall in love," I said. "I'm not too changeable."

"I never thought I was," Chicago said, flipping over on her stomach. "Hey, Suzy, do you know what I got Roger for a graduation present?"

"What?"

"An identification bracelet. It's at Hanlon's being engraved."

I said, "Neat," enthusiastically, but I felt a little lonely and left out, too.

"There's only one word on it," Chicago said. "It's STRETCH."

"As in reach?"

"As in reach up and try to get it. Always. That's what I want him to do."

"Yeah, but sometimes it can backfire."

147

"With a little help from your friends, and sister," she said snidely.

"I'm sorry I went through your knapsack."

"I just wish you'd had a reason or a cause, or something besides that damned curiosity of yours. I could have forgiven you easier if you were doing it for something you believed in. You don't have any social consciousness, either."

"I guess not," I said. "I'm sorry I got you into this mess."

Chicago said, "No, I got me into it. And I'll get me into a lot worse, probably, in my lifetime. I'm not going to sleepwalk my way through life, not me."

"Let me ask you something, though," I said. "Aren't you sleepwalking when it comes to not recognizing how black girls feel about whites going after their boy friends?"

"Oh, I don't blame them for being mad. I'd be mad. But anger isn't constructive, Suzy. They should put that energy into changing themselves."

"Bleaching themselves or what?"

"Oh, very funny."

"Well, what exactly would you suggest?"

"They should be more feminine."

I didn't believe my ears. I was speechless.

"I know how that sounds coming from me. I've already grown my hair, or haven't you noticed?"

"I noticed."

"Suzy, I am going to become more feminine, because

black men need to prove their manhood more than white men do. They need women to lean on them because for so long they had to lean on their women. Their women got the jobs, and held the families together and were the strength, and that's got to be reversed."

"Chicago," I said, "may I ask you something?"

"Sure."

"You won't get mad?"

"No."

"Don't you think you ought to leave black men and women to solve their own problems together, their own way?"

"Ideally," she said, sounding just like Mother.

"But?"

"But I can't turn around now."

"Did you even try?"

"No," she admitted. "There was never any way. Since I first saw him, there never was any way to turn around."

She sighed and then she said, "From now on in my life, I'm going to risk a lot. Once you've decided that, you don't fear anything."

"What do you mean, you're going to risk a lot? What are you going to risk?"

"Whatever I have to."

"To do what?"

"To help start making things even," she told me. "To help people realize their own worth, the ones who don't even suspect they have any. I'm going to teach them about revolution, about getting what's coming to them, about how to fight the pigs who keep them down."

It was hard for me to trust in what she was saying because she was still very much Chicago—sounding off from the upstairs bedroom with the ocean view, lying atop Porthault sheets with the Slade monogram stitched on them with gold thread, languishing with me in our room with the built-in color TV, the best hi-fi equipment money could buy, and a special screen and projector to show our own home movies on. She smelled of Mother's perfume, which Mother once said was the most expensive in the entire world.

"Chicago?"

"What?"

"Are you going back to calling yourself Priscilla?"

"I wish the only two nicknames for Priscilla weren't Pris and Cilly," she said, smiling. "But you're right. I've been thinking of taking back my real name."

We watched each other's eyes for a slow second and then her face was strangely shy-looking. I'd never seen that expression on Chicago's face before.

She said, "I want to be a woman for him, Suzy. I've never felt this way before: that I want to be a woman."

"Your hair looks really neat," I said. It was such a stupid remark; I wished I could have thought of something better to say, something she'd always remember like I'd always remember her telling me she wanted to be a woman.

But suddenly on that summery afternoon toward evening I was close to Chicago the way I'd always imagined sisters were, and we could talk with each other. Even though we weren't at all alike, and I couldn't quite go along with her new self, as she couldn't take to my old self, I think we loved each other finally.

Mother was flirting with Daddy all through dinner that night. Chicago whispered to me that it was outrageous, and I guess it was. But it didn't really hurt anything. I think Daddy might even have been flattered.

He went back to New York just after dark, and Mother got very drunk and cried and said her tears were tears of happiness because Daddy proved after all he did care about us.

"That's not why you're crying," said Chicago. "You're crying because what you're pulling on Dad didn't work." Chicago had had a little too much dinner wine herself.

Mother got very steamed up and shouted How dare you and Of all the nerve at the top of her lungs, and it was easy to see Chicago had touched an exposed nerve. Then Mother began to play a lot of tunes from the fifties, and I thought of poor Miss Spring playing her records all by herself. I sat there remembering how I'd gone over to her house and she thought I'd come to give her comfort, and I felt bad. I drifted off into a guilty daydream of punishment and repentance, coming to only when another

151

flare-up between Mother and Chicago developed into a shouting fight.

"After all the analysis you've had, you don't know yourself at all!" said Chicago.

"I know myself well enough to know I'm not some cheap little exhibitionist!" my mother shouted back.

"What does *that* mean?"

"It means I know myself well enough to know I don't need attention so badly I'd go to any length to get it!"

"What are you trying to tell me?" Chicago demanded.

"That you don't love anyone!" said my mother. "That you love only yourself and your image as someone people will point out on the street and whisper about. You don't care about revolution and you don't care about that black boy! You love the stir you're causing, the feathers you're ruffling, the spotlight! That's what you love and what you've always loved!"

Chicago stormed from the house, grabbing the flashlight off the chest in the hallway as she went. We could see her heading past the solarium window, going down toward the beach.

I made a start to follow her.

"Let her go," said Mother in a tired tone.

"I think you're wrong," I said.

"I could be."

"I know you're wrong about her feeling for Roger," I said. "You shouldn't have said that."

"I know I shouldn't have," my mother said, "and I

wouldn't have if it was a perfect world without blemish. But it's an imperfect world and we all operate under handicaps, and one of mine is impatience. I just don't feel up to going through this particular stage of Chicago's."

"She's going through something, too, you know."

"She won't be for long."

"Mother, she's in love, and she might even *be* a serious revolutionary. I mean, how many serious revolutionaries have we ever met?"

"That isn't what I mean," said my mother. "What I mean is her young Robin Hood has agreed not to see her again."

"I don't believe that."

"Well, it's true. It's a condition of his bail, mutually agreed on by your father and his grandfather . . . and Roger."

"Roger wouldn't agree to that."

"He already has."

"Then he was forced to!"

"Hush." My mother put a finger to her lips in a gesture to silence me. "No more about it now," she said firmly. Then she added in a soft voice, "You knew it was wrong. You knew that yourself. You said yourself how poor Nan felt."

We sat there in the dark awhile, listening to an old Elvis Presley record. I knew Mother was feeling bad herself, but as usual I couldn't think of anything to say to make it better.

At the sound of the first cries, we both sat forward, both of us giving each other did-you-hear-what-I-heard looks. Then we heard another outcry, and another, and by then we were on our feet and running. Mother was calling for Macaulay, and I was running ahead, and pretty soon we were all stumbling through the sand in the light of the moon, in the direction of Chicago's screams.

There were five or six black girls running from the scene. They must have been posted outside our house, perhaps many nights in a row, waiting for the moment.

They had shaved off all of Chicago's hair.

She was sitting there holding her head, crying like a baby. I began to cry, too, remembering how proudly she'd told me growing her hair was the beginning of becoming more feminine.

Mother sat on the dunes between us and put her arms around us both, and held us the way she never had when we were little kids.

She told Macaulay to go on back to the house. She said she could take care of it.

Eighteen

My sister went into New York City the next morning to buy a wig. Mother went with her. Macaulay drove them.

They must have been at Elizabeth Arden just about the time Roger came strolling into the library.

"What's he doing loose?" Mrs. Timberlake exclaimed. "And what's he doing here of all places, returning to the scene of the crime?"

"He's out on bail," Miss Spring informed her.

"Well, what's he doing *here*?"

There was no answer from Miss Spring or me. The three of us just gaped at Roger as he walked straight for us, unsmiling, his eyes harder than I had remembered them. His voice when he spoke was aggressive and loud enough for Mrs. Timberlake to interject.

"Did Nan get blamed?"

"Shhhhh. Young man, this is a library!"

"Was she charged with anything?"

"Tell him about Nan, Suzy," said Miss Spring.

I said, "Roger, come on with me," and I led him through

155

the side door to a small stone patio just outside the main reading room.

I said, "Chicago's in New York."

He looked at me with no expression on his face. He said, "How did Nan come out?"

"I just thought I'd tell you where Chicago is, first, and what happened to her."

"I heard," Roger said.

"It was really rough on her," I said.

"What happened to Nan?"

"I don't think anything's going to happen to her. Not as far as the library's concerned."

"And the police?"

"So far they've just said she should be around if they have to question her," I said. "But she's still not going to school."

He looked at me for a moment, that same lack of expression on his face. Then he shrugged his shoulders again, and I thought of how I'd been shrugging my shoulders all spring, and I asked him, almost like I was asking myself, "Doesn't that make you feel anything?"

"It's cool," he said, "if that's what she wants."

"She's working as a waitress," I said.

He said, "Cool," and shrugged again.

I said, "Maybe you can't feel anything." I was still talking to myself.

Roger said, "Feeling all over the place isn't feeling anything."

156

"What does that mean?"

"You have to choose, Suz. Choose a side on which to ride."

"Chicago's my sister," I said, "and Nan's a good friend. I don't see how I could choose."

"Then you belong on the sidelines watching, with the vast majority."

"Did you choose?" I asked. "It's not my sister, is it?"

He gave me a distant little salute of farewell, turned away, and walked back through the library, out the front door.

Miss Spring came out to get me, because I was taking my time going back to Check Out.

"Are those tears in your eyes, Mama-doodle?"

"I feel bad for my sister."

"Because now he wants Nan back?"

"I don't know for sure," I said, "but I don't think he wants my sister."

"Maybe your sister doesn't want him now, either. She can go back to her life, and he can go back to being vale-dictorian, and probably Nan will be in school next year, too."

"Oh, my poor sister."

"You've been calling her your sister a lot suddenly," said Miss Spring.

"What do I usually call her?"

"Just Chicago."

"Oh."

Miss Spring said, "Now is as good a time as any to tell you: I'm leaving Seaville for a while."

"A vacation?" I sat down beside her on the stone bench in front of the ivy-covered brick wall in the sun. She wasn't dressing her old way at all anymore. She had on a plain brown dress, stockings, and brown Oxfords that laced. She seemed so much older to me, and more solemn.

"Yes, you may call it a vacation."

"But you'll be gone longer."

"Much longer."

"In other words you're sort of leaving."

"Sort of leaving. Yes, Mama-doodle. I should have sort of left long ago. I waited around here. It wasn't good."

"Was it bad, though?"

"I didn't think so at the time. I thought I was waiting for something. But now I see the waste."

"I wouldn't call it that," I said.

"You weren't the one doing the wasting," she said. "I was. I wasted myself in a futile fantasy. I grew wrinkles dreaming. Wrinkles should come from living, not imagining that you are."

I asked, "Where will you go?"

"I'll wander. I don't have any place to go, but I don't have any place to stay any longer, either."

I turned away my head. "I'll miss you."

"I'll miss you, too, Mama-doodle. Don't *you* forget to live."

"What do you mean?"

158

"Don't watch too much. Don't do it in your head too much."

"Gwen?" Mrs. Timberlake's voice from inside. "Here's someone to see about the Phineas Ulin position."

"We'll say a real good-by before I go, Suzy," she said.

We stood up. I looked down at her tiny eyes framed by the Coke-bottle-bottom glasses, and I couldn't smell any scent, but I remembered the odor of Tweed, and the look of frosty zombies, and I was afraid I would sob.

I started to do what Roger had done. Just say "Cool" and shrug.

Instead, I grabbed Miss Spring and hugged her hard. We both cried.

That afternoon as I walked from town out to Ocean Road, I thought a lot about the next day. It was graduation day. That very moment girls were hanging their prom dresses on the back of closet doors, and boys were coming back from the tailor with rental tuxes, making last-minute phone calls about who was going in what car. The florists were assembling corsage boxes and answering telephone orders. Patches was getting ready for a gala night, and there were long tables being set up at Tout Va Bien and Sea Side for parties of ten and twenty. All the cars the kids were driving around town were turning corners with wheels squealing, and everyone had someplace they had to be—you could feel that in the air.

I guess I would have liked Chicago to be part of it. Or

maybe that was a projection: maybe I just wished I was part of it.

Whatever I wanted for my sister, it wasn't what I felt she was going to have to face when she got back from New York.

For a while, as I walked toward the ocean and our home overlooking it, I had this fantasy of my sister and me growing older together, different from others, even a little distant where others were concerned, but living together in our house on the ocean, just the two of us, having drinks after dinner in the solarium, listening to tapes and talking about what we'd learned from life now we'd gotten older and wiser, the two Slade sisters. I remembered the afternoon we'd talked, stretched out naked on our beds, listening to the ocean slap the beach, watching the red sky and the new moon appear, caring what happened to each other like kin should.

That night I ate dinner alone, at the long dining table, served by Mrs. Leary. She tried so hard to keep some sort of frivolous conversation going between courses, so I wouldn't think about Mother's phone call.

Mother had called around six.

She'd told me: "We left Elizabeth Arden about two, to go back to the garage where Macaulay was waiting. We were on Fifth Avenue near 57th Street. Chicago smiled, a very odd smile for her because she looked deep into my eyes at the same time. She said, 'Mother, we might have ended up liking each other.' I gave a little laugh—I was

160

surprised, pleased—and then the 'might have' registered and I looked to see the expression on her face, and found her gone. . . . I'm with your father. Of course she'll come back. It's some sort of whim, a game—"

All night I kept thinking of my mother's expression, how strange it was: "found her gone."

Nineteen

Four months ago, on the same day Chicago disappeared along Fifth Avenue, Roger Coe jumped bail, too. Neither one has been seen or heard of since then.

My mother is busy working for the election of Martha Crammer's mother to town supervisor. The solarium is packed afternoons with envelope lickers and fund solicitors phoning around the village. There are angry letters to the editors in the newspaper complaining that only the rich can afford to campaign as Mrs. Crammer is, that money should not buy an election. My mother responds that wealth should not be a deterrent to an earnest desire to serve the public intelligently.

Nan Richmond's back in school. She still waits on tables evenings at Tout Va Bien, and she avoids the library, and me, as one steers clear of the enemy. When we do meet, she gives me one of her looks, and I turn my head because it hurts. I remember when she'd fake those hate faces, when we were working together, and we'd go back in the stacks to crack up, what seems now like so long ago.

My father will be a father again in three months. I went to dinner with them last month in New York. Enid had memorized something she said reminded her of Chicago, from an old interview with e.e. cummings, the poet.

To be nobody-but-myself—in a world which is doing its best, night and day, to make you everybody else—means to fight the hardest battle which any human being can fight, and never stop fighting.

My father drank too much, for a change, and cried because he said he ached so for Chicago.

I think the worst part is not knowing where she is, with whom, and what she is doing or planning.

My mother said it would be almost easier if she were dead, then clapped her hand across her mouth as though God could hear and would immediately act on it, to show her what people got who said such things.

I wear the I.D. bracelet that Chicago never picked up from Hanlon's, the one with STRETCH written across it, the one she bought for Roger.

Weekly the detectives report, and weekly reassure Mother that there are thousands and thousands of young-sters missing, that Chicago is by no means the only one, and four months after all is not a year or two years.

There have been cases—

Sometimes Mother sits in the solarium sipping bourbon and wondering softly to herself, in whispery murmurs cracked with emotion, "If only I knew that she was with someone . . . with him . . . with someone watching over her. Or that she was even alive. Oh, my baby."

There was this postcard last week from Miss Spring:

> *Mama-doodle!*
> *I have thought over what L.Q. had to say to me and believe he is sick himself, too proud to let me see him sink. Returning very soon. Spirits high! G.S.*

My mother said, "So she's back in her rut, hah?"

I said, "I guess it's hard to change when you're older."

"Don't worry, pet," said my mother. (She's taken to calling me pet for some reason, perhaps because like the good old faithful sheepdog I am always here and can be counted on.) "Don't you worry. It's hard to change when you're younger, too, and if you've been spoiled rotten all your life like Chicago was. She's not having an easy time of it!"

My mother's fond of repeating, "She'll be home as soon as it gets cold."

I don't like to think of Chicago coming back just for that reason.

I think Mother's trying to convince herself, more than she's stating something she's sure about.

It's been lonely without Chicago, even though she was

163

living here in my room with me for such a short time. I miss seeing Roger strolling around town on his long legs, too. I remember his smile, and his greetings: "What's the news, Suz?" "What's the story, Morning Glory?"

Because we can't even guess their whereabouts, I can't imagine what they're doing, any more than I can fathom what they think they're doing, or what's to become of them. I picture them sometimes, speeding along on Roger's bike down sunny country highways, their heads full of daring plans to change the world, close and safe and happy. Other times, I see them sharing some scant and greasy meal, late at night in some run-down big city café, anonymous and broke, getting sick of each other's company—wondering what it is they've gotten themselves into.

Maybe the truth is somewhere in between.

Wherever they are, and I think of them always as being together, I hope they're not cold.

THE END

Format by Joyce Hopkins
Set in 12 pt. Granjon
Composed, printed and bound by The Haddon Craftsmen, Inc.
HARPER & ROW, PUBLISHERS, INCORPORATED